THE TRUTH OF HONOR

HONOR TRILOGY: BOOK 2

FoxTales Press

LYRA THORSSON

CHAPTER ONE

Rebecca

"You will always be *meine Liebchen*."

My eyes shot open. I glanced around, breathing quickly, trying to ground myself. Gray walls, simple furniture, a full-sized bed, a door leading to a bathroom. None of it felt familiar, and yet it all did.

I couldn't be back here—I couldn't be back in the military, or he would get to me. I had to get out of here. I had to leave right now.

My brain kept screaming at me to run as I took in a

deep breath and let it out slowly. First I needed to try to remember where I was. What was the last thing I remembered? Nik, Jonathan, and Admiral Bardon. That was right—we were given a mission to take down Admiral Sebastien Wilde. And we did. Or at least I was able to lead Admiral Bardon to one of Sebastien's facilities where he was experimenting on innocent people, trying to create the perfect weapon.

I took a few deep breaths as I reached for the vials I kept at my bedside—a little morphine-B I had been taking since before we ran away three years ago. I should have gone to a doctor earlier to get the shot that would make my body not fall into withdrawal, but we were too afraid we would get turned in even if we weren't in the Nreff Nation territory. It was also too expensive for me to grab on the black market, and I couldn't exactly tell Nik I was an addict. He wouldn't understand. Now it didn't matter—now we were in the clear.

Thankfully, even in all my years of getting the drug on the black market, I never had to take the normal morphine. If I had, then I would have to keep upping my dose until I overdosed. With morphine-B, I didn't have to worry about it as doctors had perfected the formula so the body didn't ever require more, nor was it as harmful to my organs. I was still addicted to it, however, and needed the shot to get off of it. But that wouldn't be until tomorrow and right now I needed something to take the edge off.

With my hand shaking, I opened the vial and took the entire dose—the bitter, almost acidic substance burning on the way down. It tasted vile, but at this point I didn't care anymore. I just needed it to calm down.

I pulled my legs into my chest and leaned my forehead against my knees. Gently rocking back and forth, I let the tears wash away the aching feeling I had in my heart.

"It's okay," I whispered. "He's in jail now. He can't get to me. I am safe."

I knew it was a lie. I knew that no matter where he was in this universe, he would still have a way to get to me. I was never safe. I never would be safe.

My breathing rate began to increase, and I squeezed my eyes shut. Why did things have to be like this? Why did I make such stupid decisions when I was seventeen? Sixteen years later, I was still paying the price. I tried to take a deep breath through my mouth, but my lips quivered and it came out in an anguished gasp.

When would the drugs kick in?

Even in my peril, my mind was smart enough not to grab another bottle. It would just take a moment since the drug had to be absorbed through my digestive system. It wasn't as quick as smoking or a needle, but after everything I had been through, there was no way I was going to be able to inject myself. I hated needles. I hated being in a doctor's office.

Which was going to make later that day even more difficult to deal with.

But I had to go to the doctor and get off this medicine. Then I could finally move on with my life. It was making the memories worse—it was making me feel as if I couldn't move on without it. Once I was off of it, then I could work on everything else.

Once I was clean, I would feel less weak.

My body felt a little more relaxed, and I took another deep breath, letting my entire body melt. Even though I didn't like being on this drug, I wasn't sure how I would have survived after everything that happened three years earlier.

When that bastard killed my fiancé.

My heart began to race again. I shouldn't have thought about Walrum—I should have just leaned back and gone to sleep so my dreams could remind me of my pain.

It felt like yesterday when I walked into the room and found him sprawled out in his cell—beaten and bloody. Jonathan and Nik had checked his pulse and found he was dead.

That was the day I felt as if I had died—the day I knew everyone around me was going to be destroyed if I didn't run away.

More tears were falling. But that wasn't the end. Sebastien wouldn't let me just suffer the fact that my fiancé was dead. No—he had done horrendous things to Walrum's body—creating a monster.

I didn't know how he had done it. No one had. They were still running tests on him. I wasn't even sure if the real Walrum was still in there.

But he was dead. We saw it with our own eyes.

When Sebastien had revealed him to me a couple of weeks ago, I had snapped. It was the only time I had ever attacked Sebastien other than the two times I had slapped him. Nik had to pull me off of him when they had raided the facility.

I had never been so furious—I had never wanted to kill him as much as I did at that moment. Fear had been overtaken by pure anger. I wished Nik hadn't intervened—I probably would have killed him. And that sick fuck was laughing the entire time.

The drug was taking a better hold, and I felt the drowsiness engulf me once again. I fell back on my pillow, and darkness swallowed me up. If only it would swallow me up forever.

I woke up a few hours later, in less distress but still shaken and wondering what was in store for me that day. Knowing my luck, probably something disastrous. That was how it always was, but I kept moving forward —it was the only thing I could do at that point.

Stepping into the shower, I let the hot water relax my body. When Nik and I were on the run, we didn't exactly have a real shower on our ship, and all the hotels we stayed at were pretty cheap and always had cold water. I could get used to a nice place like this, which really wasn't that nice. It was just military hospitality rooms for the higher-ranking officers. I used to be a captain after all.

After a nice long shower, I changed into my normal tank and cargo pants. I liked having the pockets, and it was a rather warm day on Regenswelt—which meant it was humid as well. This planet was always so wet, hence the name. It was the capital planet of the Nreff Nation and where Sebastien's trial would take place. I wanted to leave, but I had to give my testimony or whatever. I wasn't sure how that was going to go down and still needed to discuss specifics with Admiral Bardon, but I had been putting it off until after I visited with the doctor, which I had also been putting off.

Running my fingers through my short red hair, I headed out toward the commons to grab a bite to eat. It was packed with officers. I glanced around but didn't see any sign of Nik or Jonathan. I grabbed some grapes and nuts since that was all I could find to eat and took a seat by myself at a small table.

The grapes weren't the best quality, but it was pretty good for military food. I sighed as I glanced around. How many of these officers knew what was going on under their noses? How many of them worked for Sebastien and were watching my every move? How many were just cocky men who thought becoming a military officer would get them laid?

As I almost finished the grapes and seeds, I heard a few men talking behind me.

"Do you see those scars on her? What the heck?"

I glanced down at my arms. They weren't the only parts of me that were scarred. I didn't care how I appeared any longer nor who stared at them. They were visual indicators of how I felt on the inside—marked and forever changed.

"I'd still fuck her though. Do you see those curves?"

I stood up and turned to glare at them. The three boys froze. If we weren't in a crowded area, I would have probably knocked some sense into them—a few punches here and there—but I didn't need more eyes on me than necessary.

Glancing at the clock, I found that it was time to head to the clinic before I was late for my appointment. All I needed was for them to tell Admiral Bardon I had skipped getting the shot. Again.

As I made my way across the facility, doubt and fear crept deeper and deeper into my mind. What if the doctor treating me was associated with Sebastien? What if they drugged me and I woke up on a table to be tortured and experimented on? My heart began to race. I shook my head as I walked. No, that wouldn't be possible. He had no power currently; he couldn't get to me.

At least not that way.

I dug my nails into the skin on my arm, careful not to draw blood as I knew the doctor would ask what happened. Or, perhaps, nail marks appeared more suspicious. If they started bleeding, I could say I snagged my arm on something.

Instead, I glanced up at the blue sky. Since Nik and I traveled quite often in space, I didn't get to see the sky as often as I would like, although I did prefer the freedom that space provided. The sky was beautiful, and it felt warm on my skin, although a little sticky, I had to admit.

All the military facilities were laid out the same, so I didn't have to think too much about where to go. It was all ingrained in my brain after years and years serving this nation. I even went to high school at a military facility, much to my parents' dismay. It was a good thing I knew how to forge signatures even back then.

The medical wing was in sight now, and every cell in my body felt as if it was screaming. I wanted to run and hide and never open the door for anyone. But someone would find me—they always found me in the end. Even after three years, Admiral Bardon found us.

But I could probably hide for at least a year, maybe more, if I really tried.

Before I could make up my mind, a familiar face stepped out of the medical wing.

"Oh hey, Nik."

His good eye widened as he smiled. "Becca! What are you here for?"

Right. He didn't know. "Oh, just a checkup. Maybe reduce some of these scars." I sort of moved my arms as if showing him something he already knew and probably memorized all the times we had been alone together. "What are you doing here?"

He pointed at the eye that was under the eyepatch. "Getting this fixed finally. I was going to surprise you, but the doctor said it should be healed up with one more treatment, so probably next week."

"That's amazing! I'm glad they were able to fix it."

"Yeah."

We stood there in awkward silence. This was how all our interactions went since the shit show went down. After finding out my fiancé was still alive, things got… complicated. And neither of us wanted to talk about it or our feelings, so we ignored it, just like best friends who slept together did.

"Well," I began, glancing around, "I probably should get going."

"Yeah, good luck."

With that, I left him outside, cursing at myself for not bringing up what we needed to discuss yet again.

CHAPTER TWO

Nik

Well, that was more awkward than it should have been.

I sighed, knowing one of these days I needed to tell her the truth of how I felt. I was going to after the mission was over. I really was. I had planned this great confession and how I was going to use the money we'd gotten for turning in Admiral Wilde, but that all changed when we'd found out Walrum was still alive. Now the words wouldn't come.

Heading toward the offices, I went to meet with

Bardon and Jonathan. We had some matters to discuss about Walrum—ones that Bardon said he was going to hold off telling Becca since she was tied to him—not to mention she was never part of our original mission.

It was a nice day today, which was always strange after two weeks of straight rain. It made it humid, however, and I was glad I'd found a tank and some shorts to wear, otherwise I would be sweating something fierce. I nodded to younger officers as they ran past, heading to training. I did not miss those days —nor did I like remembering how many years ago that was. Was it twenty years now since I graduated from the academy? I did not like the sound of that.

I should be retired by now. I should have been able to save up enough to buy some remote cottage on a lake and just waste away for the rest of my life. But all that went out the window the moment Admiral Wilde set us up and tried to make it appear we'd murdered a representative from Nash Mir, a planet not too far from here. He had figured out we were sent by Admiral Bardon to spy on him. The problem was, there shouldn't have been any trail back to him, so how did he know?

Perhaps that was what today's meeting was about. I

wanted answers, and I felt that Bardon and Jonathan were keeping things from me, as they had been a couple for quite some time now—apparently since we graduated from the academy. Perhaps Wilde found out about that, and that was why he'd set us up. One never knew with Wilde. It could have just been a whim. He was a monster, so I wouldn't put it past him.

Arriving at the admiral's offices, I saluted and showed my ID. The lieutenant scanned it and let me proceed inside. I felt out of my element, even after all the years I'd served. Three years on the run from all military, no matter the nation or zone, did that to one. I still felt as if someone were going to murder me in my sleep for what all the newscasts said about me, mainly that I murdered one of the most beloved representatives in the nation, but once the mission was finished, Admiral Bardon went on record saying we were exonerated from any crimes. I had a feeling, however, that not everyone agreed and that I was still a target in some people's eyes. I was used to people wanting me dead, however, so I wasn't going to worry about it too much.

Admiral Bardon and Jonathan were already in the conference room. Admiral Bardon's curly graying hair appeared as disheveled as always. Next to Jonathan and his own messy brown hair that was gelled back, they appeared like two peas in a pod. Although I didn't care they were in a relationship, it still weirded me out that one of my best friends was dating our old commander from when we were teenagers. And he had been keeping it from me for almost two decades. And he was almost old enough to be our dad. But I ignored that bit as best I could. To each their own, and they were happy. It warmed my heart, seeing the way they looked at each other, and I wished I could do the same with the person I loved.

I saluted to Admiral Bardon.

He waved for me to be dismissed. "You don't need to do that when we are alone. I know you want out of this place," Bardon said as he nodded toward the door. "Close the door behind you."

I nodded and did as he asked. "Never know who is watching. I don't need any of the other admirals chewing me out."

"So you aren't going to deny that you want out of this place?"

"It has crossed my mind."

Bardon smiled. "I can't blame you. I wanted to leave,

but my desire to see Sebastien taken down was greater."

"As it was for me. But now that he is behind bars with his trial date coming up, perhaps we will both get our dream to come true." I took a seat. "Unless you think he won't be tried fairly."

Jonathan and Bardon glanced at each other. I let out a defeated laugh. "You have to be kidding me. We found the facility."

Bardon sighed. "We did. And he's claiming that he had no idea it was there and didn't have a part in it. All the doctors we arrested are saying they have never met Sebastien before."

I shook my head. "*Scheiße. Ernsthaft?* We were there! We know it was him!"

Jonathan shrugged. "*Je connais.* Apparently it's not enough to hold up in court."

I slammed my hand on the table. "We made Becca go through all that! We can't just let him walk away freely."

Bardon tapped on the table. "I know. She could give her testimony, but I'm afraid he would drag her down with him. She will have to be careful what she says, and I don't know if I can ask her to do that."

I shook my head. "She had nothing to do with the

things that he did. We would know— I would know…"

Bardon and Jonathan glanced at each other. Bardon coughed. "Even if she hadn't, anything she said he would spin on her. She can give her testimony of what had just happened, but it would be her word against his, not to mention he would try to say she is emotionally unstable due to finding her fiancé. For now, we can't use her."

This was getting more and more frustrating by the minute. "How is Walrum? Have they found out anything yet?"

Bardon shrugged. "We know he has been worked on. Dr. Mostovoi has been working on him since it is her area of expertise. But I don't think there has been any progress on reversing it or getting him to remember anything."

Part of me was glad, which made me even more disgusted with myself. I should want my friend back— he didn't deserve what happened to him. He was wrongfully accused and then killed for the actions of a madman. He should have been alive, and he and Becca should have been happily married.

But part of me wanted her in my arms. Who was I kidding? I fully wanted her in my arms, but if Walrum was back in the picture, that meant there was a chance he could come back to us, and she would go back to him.

At least, that was what I thought.

I really needed to talk to her, but I didn't want to hear those words—the words saying she wanted to be with Walrum. I let out a slow breath.

"So we are up shit creek without a paddle."

"*Ne t'inquiète pas*. We just need more evidence before the trial. I am having my people try to follow strings, so to speak, which means I might need you on a mission coming up. Are you ready for that?" Bardon asked.

I nodded. "Of course. Anything to get that *Schwein* behind bars. Just tell me what I need to do."

"Good. You will have to go without Rebecca, just in case," Bardon explained.

I narrowed my good eye. "In case of what?"

He shrugged. "We just don't know, Nik. We don't know who is stuck in Sebastien's web—this is way bigger than we could ever imagine. The fact that none of those doctors—none of the staff—will confess, even with the threat of being in prison for the rest of their lives, is frightening. He has them all wrapped around his finger, and I don't know how much we can convince them otherwise."

I glanced between the two of them. "You can't be serious. We served with her. I have been on the run with her for over three years! There is no way she is serving Sebastien. She just helped us take him into custody."

"She did. But he is one twisted fuck, and for all we know, she could be acting. Or he is using her as a puppet. We just have to be careful and only can trust the three of us. *Vous comprenez*? Anything discussed here is not to leave this room."

Jonathan tried to smile innocently, but I simply glared at him. He knew as well as I that there was no way she could be helping him—not after everything we had gone through.

"If she was a part of it, then why would she have been part of the mission that was sabotaged by Wilde? Why would he have tortured her like that?"

Bardon shrugged. "Sebastien makes no sense to me either. He's sadistic and a sociopath. Why would he think it was all right to perform experiments on people? Because he's crazy. But he's also smart and likes to weave webs that not even I can seem to unravel. Just promise me you won't tell her what we discuss. After it is all over, then you can confess to your heart's content. But until then, we need to find more evidence and take him down."

I gritted my teeth. She should have been included—she was practically a part of our mission. We had served with her almost the entire time since we were recruited by Bardon to spy on Wilde. She joined us five years after we began.

"Fine. *Was immer*. But you are wrong. She isn't a spy for him."

"I don't believe she is a willing spy, Nik. If she is working for him, it would be unwillingly and he would have something on her. I just want to keep her—and us —safe from that. Don't you want her safe?"

I nodded. "*Ja*, I do. I won't tell her. I wouldn't go against orders anyway. But I trust her with my life. I want that on record."

Bardon studied me for a moment, then smiled. "Ah, I see. You two are sleeping together."

Jonathan started laughing. I gave him a look, then turned back to Bardon.

"Not… technically? We were, but then…"

"But then her dead fiancé is actually alive but isn't because he is brainwashed by her other ex. Got it."

I frowned. It was a lot more complicated than I wanted to admit, but that summed it up. I just wanted her to be happy. After everything she had been through, she deserved it. I didn't care what anyone else said.

Bardon nodded to my eyepatch. "How are treatments going? For your eye."

"Good. I think I will be able to take the eyepatch off soon."

"*Ça c'est bon.*"

"*Danke.* Is there anything else you need from me?" I asked. I had skipped breakfast, and my stomach was reminding me of that decision.

Bardon shook his head. "No. That will be all. I'll let you know once I have a mission for you. You will need to check out if you go into the city, but otherwise you are free."

I nodded and stood up. I felt like saluting, but he had mentioned I didn't need to do that. It felt odd, so I did sort of a half nod and hurried out the door to go find myself something to eat.

CHAPTER THREE

Rebecca

Doctors were always late, even in a small facility like this one. My knee bounced as I slouched in the uncomfortable waiting chair. I folded my arms in front of me and checked the clock. It was five minutes slow, and it was ten past my appointment time. How could they be late this early in the morning? I was the second appointment for the day.

I wanted to take slow, deep breaths, but then I would get a big whiff of the chemical smell that always filled medical units. I hated the smell. I could go my entire life without smelling that horrific smell ever again.

Digging my nails into my skin, I tried not to think of the last time I was on a medical table. It was when Sebastien kidnapped me. That was still fresh in my mind since it was within the past two weeks. My nails went deeper into my skin.

"Rebecca Kompen?" A nurse stepped into the waiting room. She was tall—taller than me—with dyed silver hair back in a messy bun. She stared at me over her thick-rimmed glasses. I glanced around. There was literally no one else here.

I stood up. "Unfortunately."

"Right this way. I am going to take your vitals, and then the doctor will be with you."

I nodded. "Right."

The medical room was typical—small, had some photos of space, landscapes, and smiling people. There were a couple of chairs and the dreaded cushion table thing. Of course, there was also a tablet and other scanners.

"Please take a seat on the table."

I shook my head. "I'm going to sit in the chair, if you don't mind."

The nurse didn't even blink. "That's fine. Now, can you answer a few questions for me while I take your blood pressure and heart rate?"

"Sure." I sat down on the crappy chair and held out my arm. She put a wrist blood pressure reader and a cap that went over my finger.

"According to your chart, you had the hysterectomy when you got out of the academy."

"*Ja.*"

"Are you sexually active?"

"I… uh, kinda? Sure."

"Bowel movements?"

"Fine."

"Do you drink or smoke?"

"*Nein.*"

"Are you on any drugs?"

"I… uh, shouldn't the reason I'm here be in that chart of yours?"

She scanned over it. "Ah. I see." She made some notes and then checked the screen for my heart rate and blood pressure. "Your heart rate and blood pressure are a little high."

Well, yeah. I'm here. "Oh." I didn't know what to say —it's not like I could really explain all my nervousness to her, not to mention didn't everyone feel nervous at the doctor's?

"Let me take your temperature, and we will be all set."

She placed a device in my ear, and after a few seconds, it beeped. "All good. The doctor will be in shortly."

The nurse left me, and I glanced around the room. I hated waiting, especially in a place like this. I feared the silence, swearing I could hear his whispers.

I tried to distract myself by examining the pictures. One was of a lake on Regenswelt, just south of here. I had been there a while back with my crewmates. I remembered what fun we had that summer day, playing in the water. I had shoved Jonathan off the boat, and he ended up dragging me in with him. Walrum was smiling and having fun.

So this picture wasn't relaxing. It just brought back memories that were once joyful but now hurt more than anything. I didn't want to be reminded of Walrum and the state he was in. I didn't like being here and having to deal with interviews and seeing his progress, if there was any.

Especially since I knew the truth.

Before I could keep on wallowing in misery, the door opened. I always felt awkward being out of my chair when someone walked in, so I fumbled around a little.

The doctor—a woman about my age with curly black hair—held out her hand. "I am Dr. Theissi. Nice to meet you, Captain Kompen."

"I'm not really a captain anymore. You can call me Rebecca." I took her hand and shook it.

"All right, Rebecca, please take a seat."

I sat back down in the uncomfortable chair. My hands were shaking. I wasn't ready for this. I didn't want to have the one thing that helped me sleep be taken away.

Dr. Theissi looked over my chart on her tablet. "Can you tell me a little more about the drug you have been taking and what it was for?"

I gulped. "I got injured on one of my missions and was given some morphine-B. Then we were set up to take the fall for the rep on Nash Mir and were arrested. I didn't get the injection before I ran away and never went to a doctor for fear they would report it or that someone would find out who we were. Even in different territories, someone might recognize us. That was three years ago."

"That is a long time to be on morphine-B. Normally

when we give this shot, it helps with short-term effects of addiction. I am not sure how it is going to interact with your body, and we will have to monitor it. Where were you getting your doses?"

I hesitated. "Underground. But I tested each one to make sure it was the correct strain."

"How often were you taking a dose?"

"I take it once a day, if that, but sometimes twice if I need it."

"Do you take it for pain, or is your body craving it? Or do you take it for another reason?"

I wasn't sure how to answer that. If I told her it was for PTSD, she would make me see a therapist, and there was no way I was going to tell anyone what happened for a few reasons. "Cravings. My body starts to shake, and I can't concentrate."

The doctor tapped her tablet. "All right. It might take a few doses of the serum then. We will have to monitor you. I need you to come in for a checkup twice a day, and if you feel off, you come straight here, all right? I don't want you to have to take any more doses, but if you do, I want to monitor how much you are taking and do it here."

I didn't like the sound of that. I would have to come

here twice a day? But I also wanted to be off this drug. I wanted to be able to drink and hang out with my friends.

"All right. I can do that."

"First I am going to take some blood for tests so we can monitor your functions and how much is in your blood. When was the last time you took a dose?"

"This morning around two."

She wrote that down in the tablet and then went out of the room to grab some supplies. I clutched the fabric on my pants. I didn't want any needles—I didn't want to see them or feel them in my skin. I clenched my eyes shut and tried to take long, deep breaths. I was stronger than this. No little needle would get the better of me. I was in control of my body.

That was a lie, and I knew it.

After everything that had happened, I would never belong to myself until that bastard was dead. I felt like I wasn't in control—as if everything I did was strings being pulled by some master, and that master was Sebastien. But this would be one step in the right direction.

I should have killed him when I had the chance. But Nik and the others had stopped me. I wish they hadn't even if it meant I would have gone to jail for a long time. I was probably going to anyway.

The doctor came back in, and I opened my eyes to find her with a needle and some vials. I would not puke. I could not puke.

"Would you like to lie down on the table? I know that makes it easier for some people."

"No," I answered quickly. I definitely did not want to be lying down.

"Okay, stick your arm out please."

I did as she asked, and she wiped the alcohol on my skin. She wrapped a piece of rubber around my arm and I looked away as she stuck the needle in. There was a slight pinch, but it wasn't the pain that I hated—it was all the memories that came flooding back. I took long breaths, counting to ten in and counting ten out.

"All done."

I turned to find she had a few vials of blood filled. I leaned back a little more, trying to make my eyes not become dizzy. My stomach was getting a little angry, but I could handle it.

"We will have those run, but it should only take fifteen minutes. I'll need to run blood work again tomorrow to see how it has changed. Does the same time work?"

I nodded. "*Ja*, I don't have anything going on."

"Great. As for tonight, I just want you to come in here and have the nurse take your vitals and answer a few questions. It can be at any time, but our normal hours are from seven in the morning to nine at night. So come in after dinner."

"Okay." I really didn't want to, but it didn't look like I had a choice.

"And if there is an emergency, just come straight in. Do not hesitate to call us for anything, all right? I don't want you to second-guess yourself."

It would be bad if I needed to come in. "I will."

"Let me go and get the serum then." She got up and took the blood with her. It shouldn't take long, but I also didn't want to wait here.

I leaned back for a bit, staring at the ceiling, waiting for the dizziness to subside. I hated that I was alone, and yet there wasn't anyone whom I wanted to tell the truth to. It wasn't like I could let Nik know I had been on this drug for so long, especially since I had kept it from him all this time. At first it was because I was too afraid to go to the doctor, and then it was the fact that I didn't want to get rid of the only thing that calmed me down when I thought about Sebastien and what he had done. Then I would have had to tell him everything.

To be honest, I didn't want to stop taking it. I wanted to be able to sleep at night. Without this, what was I going to do? Go and murder him once and for all and not have to worry? It was a possibility if it weren't for the fact he was heavily guarded. Even with my clearance I doubt I would get away with it.

Besides, that wasn't how this was going to play out. No, I had to finish what I started, and then I could be free. Then I could kill him.

Fifteen minutes passed, and the doctor finally came back in with the serum.

"The results show that your organs are functioning normally, which was surprising given how long you have been on the drug."

"I'm just lucky, I guess." I really wasn't.

"I am going to inject your other arm. It might be a little sore, so be sure to move it around. Some people get tired or just feel off, but it will only be for a couple of hours. Otherwise, you can go about a normal day."

She wiped another alcohol cloth on my other arm and injected the needle. Seconds later, she was done.

"Am I good to go now?" I asked.

"Just one more thing. Admiral Bardon requested I give you the numbers of some therapists to talk to. After everything, you really do need to talk to someone. It will help you get back to life before—"

"I'm fine." I stopped her before she could go on. "I have had a lot of time to think and deal with the shit I have been through, and I don't need someone else telling me what to feel."

She pursed her lips. "All right. But just in case, I'm still giving you the numbers. Do as you like. I can't force you. But it may help you get through the real reason you have been taking morphine-B."

She handed me the list. I glanced at it and almost chuckled when I saw one of the names on it. A session with him actually might be what I needed, but I would never admit that to him.

"*Danke*. Can I leave now?"

"Yes. Just be sure to check in later tonight."

I nodded and left the medical wing as quickly as I could.

CHAPTER FOUR

Nik

"Oh *zdravstvuy*, Nik," Alexandra, or Dr. Mostovoi, greeted in Russian as I stepped into the facility that was keeping Walrum.

I had finished my breakfast, and it was eating at me to see what was going on. I had read the report summaries from Jonathan, but other than when I first came here, I hadn't actually gone to see him. He was violent then, thrashing around like some angry animal. They had said he hadn't improved too much, but I needed to see it for myself.

"*Hallo*, Alexandra. I'm just checking in."

Alexandra brushed back her red hair and smiled. "Right. Well, I was just going to take a walk around the campus for a bit. I need a break. Would you like to join me?"

I didn't have anything else to do, so I nodded. "Sure. But after, can I see him?"

"Of course. But first I can fill you in on everything."

I followed her back outside. She unbuttoned her white doctor's jacket. "Wow, it sure is hot out today. I haven't been out for a while, so I didn't even realize."

"*Ja*, and it's only midmorning."

"This planet is so strange in its weather. It will rain for a week, and then all of a sudden it will be hotter than ever."

"And don't forget humid."

"Very, very humid. I don't know how all those cadets do it—running around in this temperature."

"You get used to it."

She turned and looked up at me. "Did you train here when you were younger?"

I acted like I was being stabbed in the heart. "Did you have to say younger? Like I am old or something?"

She laughed. "*Prosti.* I mean, when you were a teen, did you go to the academy? Or did you wait until after you graduated high school?"

I peered up at the blue sky. "I and Jonathan and Walrum all did the advanced-placement military academy. Once we graduated, an admiral could take us on, and we continued our training with the promise of being on their force."

"And Admiral Wilde selected you?"

I nodded. "Yup. We've served under him since we graduated. He didn't select many cadets. We were lucky in that way."

"And Rebecca? When did she join?"

"She also was in the advanced-placement military academy, but she is a few years younger than us. Wilde said he wasn't going to hire any more cadets from the academy, but for some reason he picked her."

"Any idea why?"

I shook my head. "Not a clue. She is good though, so perhaps he saw her potential." I glanced down at her. "Are you asking because you think it was her that you remember?"

She shrugged. "Admiral Bardon and I had a long chat about that. It was when I was very little, but that was a night that I'll never forget. I am pretty sure it was, but he assured me that I should forget about it and that the main person to blame is Admiral Wilde, whom we have in custody."

"Do you want revenge on her if it was?"

Alexandra frowned. "Having seen the things he has done and how no one at the facility will testify against him, I can't blame anyone other than him. He is good at manipulating people and getting them to do exactly want he wants."

That was definitely true. He had convinced the entire nation that they had killed a representative. "I have been with her all this time. I can't believe she would do any of that."

"And it was she who'd taken him down. Are you sure you are thinking with your mind and not with your heart?"

I blushed. "I, uh… How…?"

"It's really obvious you like her. Which is also why you came today to check on Walrum, isn't it?"

I peered down at my feet, kicking a loose rock. "You are very good at reading people."

"I don't just study the medical side of people's minds but also the psychological."

"Ah. Yeah, I did come to check on Walrum because I want to know if he is getting better. I would like my friend back or at least not suffering."

"He's… still under a lot of stress when it comes down to it. From what I can tell, the parts of the brain that were affected control his rage and anger, making him want to hurt whoever is near."

"So then they could be dropped off in enemy territory and can go berserk."

"Precisely. It is going to take some time to undo it all, but I do think it can be done. It's what my parents were working on all those years ago."

We'd made it to the edge of the camp and turned. It was strange being able to walk around there again when only three years ago I had been arrested. I wasn't sure what would happen in the end, but I knew I didn't want to stay there.

"I'm not sure if they told you, but Walrum was Rebecca's fiancé."

Her eyes widened. Apparently that information hadn't been revealed to her. "Oh. That definitely makes things complicated."

"That it does. I just don't know if I should tell her how I feel or if I should wait to see if he gets his memories back. I mean, I already felt bad that I was sleeping with his fiancé after he died, but now…" I ran my hands through my graying blond hair. "I really don't know what to do." I shook my head. "Sorry, this has nothing to do with you. It's just been on my mind constantly these past couple of weeks. I just don't want to hurt her any more than she's already been hurt."

"It's no problem. I sort of pushed you to spill—I could tell by your face you needed to talk to someone. But my advice is to tell her the truth and how you feel. You need to figure this out before both of you don't know how to bring up the conversation anymore."

She had a fair point. "Why is someone younger than me so much wiser?"

She laughed. "Because I have been trained and been studying since I was a little girl. And you're a man, so you are less wise in general."

I gave her a look, and we both started laughing. I was glad to see that she wasn't blaming Rebecca any longer, although by the sound of it, Admiral Bardon was behind that. He was the one who'd said that it was possible she was involved. I had asked him if he was going to turn her in, but it sounded like he was going to hide that from the courts. The question was, why would he go so far to do that for someone who didn't seem like she was going to confess? Did he have a soft spot for her?

We made it back to the medical facility, and Alexandra buttoned her coat back up.

"All right, do you want to see him then?"

I nodded. "Yeah. Is he awake?"

"Yes, he should be getting his lunch right about now. He's no longer acting like a wild animal, so to speak, but we have a guard on him at all times, and he is chained back. He can't hurt you."

"That's… good, I guess."

"Well, any progress is good, but I understand your hesitation. It's a shitty situation."

That was an understatement. Walrum should have been married to Becca; they should have retired from the military and lived happily ever after. But that wasn't what happened—far from it.

"*Danke*."

"Let me escort you inside. If you need anything, I'll be watching from the observation room."

She opened the door for me, and I stepped through. The room was a drab gray, as most rooms on the base were. There was a small bathroom, a chair and table, and a bed. Currently a guard stood next to where I walked in, and Walrum was sitting at the table, eating his food just as Alexandra said he would.

Walrum glanced up, his blue eyes watching me. "And who might you be?"

That stung a little. I knew he wouldn't remember me, but that didn't mean it didn't still hurt. "I'm an old friend. Just wanted to see how you are doing."

He ate more of his soup. "Well, I'm locked in here against my will, so I'm a little bit pissed off."

Contrary to what Alexandra had said, he seemed a lot more coherent than she had led on. To me, he seemed almost normal, although there was still a little violence in his eyes.

"Rightly so. But there are doctors here trying to make you better and help you regain your memory. Once that happens, you'll be a free man."

"Oh really? Do you really believe after everything that I'll be a free man? That they won't keep running tests on me, trying to figure out what I have become?"

He had a point there. But it was somewhat good that he understood what position he was in—his critical-thinking skills were better.

"Do you remember anything before we found you?" I asked as I took a seat across from him.

He clutched his spoon tightly as he stared at me. "I don't remember anything."

"Do you know who did this to you?"

Walrum shook his head. "No. I just remember some doctors and then seeing that woman attack that man when I was coherent."

He meant when Becca attacked Wilde. Part of me wished we'd gotten there later so that she would have succeeded in killing him. Then they wouldn't still be dealing with having to find proof.

"Did she look familiar to you?" I asked. "The girl who was attacking him."

"No. Should she have?"

I wasn't going to tell him the truth—or at least, not with someone ordering me to. "I suppose not. What about the man she was attacking. Did he seem familiar?"

"I can't say I've seen him before, but as I said, I don't recognize anyone."

So we couldn't quite use him as evidence against Wilde. We could at least show that there was experimentation going on.

"Is there anything else? I mean, I'm still trying to finish my lunch and all."

I shook my head when a thought occurred to me. *"Kannst du Deutsch verstehen?"*

Walrum watched me for a moment, then nodded. *"Natürlich."*

I glanced at the mirror that I knew Alexandra was behind, wondering if she already knew this. I turned back to Walrum. *"Danke."*

"Was immer." He went back to eating his soup. I nodded to the guard to open the door and found that Alexandra was already heading my way.

"We had tried speaking to him in different languages before," she said with a smile on her face. "But he hasn't ever responded. This is the first time he has spoken German."

"Really?"

She nodded quickly. "Yes. I think this might mean he is recovering slowly. Things might start coming back for him now! If you can, come visit him again tomorrow. I don't think Rebecca should come quite yet, but between you and Jonathan, I think he might regain some memories. Then we can move on from there."

"All right, I'll talk to Jonathan about it. And I'll tell him the good news about the German."

"Great. I'll see you tomorrow then."

CHAPTER FIVE

Rebecca

I stared at the salad bar, sighing. I really needed to find a place where I could cook my own food or at least a restaurant that had decent vegan meals. So far I have been thinking what flavor tofu will they serve today? It wasn't great.

Making a mental note to ask Bardon the next time I saw him for my own kitchen, I went over to the salad bar and made myself another salad. For dinner, I was definitely going to go outside the base for something.

I filled my plate and got some of the barbecued tofu for a side and found a table in the back. I still hadn't seen Jonathan or Nik that day, other than when I ran into Nik that morning. I supposed they had work to do. I knew I should check in with Bardon to see if there was any work for me, but first —deal with the drug problem.

Taking a seat, I glanced up to see I had spoken too soon—Nik and Jonathan had just stepped into the cafeteria. I debated waving to them, because I wasn't sure if I really wanted to eat with them or not, but Jonathan spotted me and waved. Looks like I wouldn't get a choice.

They went and grabbed some food. The normal meal for lunch was spaghetti and meatballs. Both of them got a plate full and sat down.

"Salad again, Bex? How boring."

I glared at him, for both the comment and for calling me Bex. I really hated that name. "I have told you countless times, I don't eat meat or anything that comes from animals."

"And I have told you countless times, meat doesn't come from animals anymore."

I stabbed my salad. "There have been numerous

reports of manufacturers substituting animals instead of lab-made meats because they are easier and cheaper. Unless you personally go to all the manufacturers and prove me wrong, I'm going to stick to my diet."

He shrugged. "To each their own, I suppose."

Nik eyed my plate. "Has that been all you really have been eating here?"

I nodded. "*Ja*. Was just about to go ask Admiral Bardon if he could give me access to a kitchen. Then I could at least have something to do."

"Well," Nik began, "until you do that, how about you and I go out tonight? Just the two of us to catch up. Seems like it has been forever since we got to just talk. You can pick the place."

Jonathan gave him a look that I couldn't quite place. I was too busy trying to figure out how to answer. There was a reason we hadn't been alone, and that was because I didn't know how I was going to explain myself to Nik. Sooner or later he was going to find out the truth about me in all this mess, and I knew it should come from me. But there was no way that was going to happen, so I had been avoiding him. I knew he wanted to talk to me about our relationship, and I wasn't sure about that either. With Walrum, everything felt odd. I didn't know what to do or say.

Especially since I knew the truth about him.

But Nik was making the initiative this time and wanted to take me to dinner. I had no real reason to refuse, and if I did, things would become even more awkward between us, and I didn't want that. "Sure. There're a few places I haven't been to in forever. Meet me at my room at six?"

He nodded. "Sounds like a plan."

Jonathan rolled his eyes but didn't say anything. "Anyway, speaking of *mon amour*, he wanted to talk to you. I think he has a few questions he wants you to clear up."

Another reason I hadn't gone to talk to Bardon about food arrangements—because then he would make me talk about everything.

"I'll go see him after this. So what have you two been up to?"

Jonathan and Nik exchanged glances. What was with all the secret codes? Did they not trust me or something? No, that couldn't be it. I had been their comrade for well over a decade. They wouldn't hide things from me would they?

Then again, I was hiding things from them, and

Bardon knew that. So it was very likely something was going on. It didn't matter though, as long as Bardon held up his end of the bargain, and Sebastien was actually thrown in jail or given the death sentence. Hopefully the latter.

But deep down, I knew what was really going to happen on the trial day. It was going to be just how Sebastien had planned it all.

"Walrum was able to speak German today," Jonathan revealed.

So it had begun. "Oh… So he's remembering."

I knew Nik was watching for a reaction, but I didn't turn to him. I didn't have a reaction because I knew what was going to happen—I knew Walrum was going to start remembering things.

Because that was exactly how Sebastien planned it.

Walrum would slowly remember, everyone would slowly trust him, and then come trial day, they were going to make their great escape. How did I know that? Because I had to help with it. I had to make sure things ran smoothly or else he would reveal to everyone how much I had a part in it all. Then I would be thrown in jail.

"Nik and I are going to visit him daily to see if he

will remember any more. Once we get the okay, you can come visit as well."

I nodded slowly. "Right. *Ja*, I can do that."

It hurt knowing that he wasn't actually getting better —that the memories he would suddenly have were the ones that Sebastien gave him and that I had helped with. I picked at my salad. I knew I should have appeared happier, but I was a mix of emotions, as any fiancée would be. Or ex-fiancée. I still wasn't sure what I was technically.

"What about you, Becca." Nik filled the awkward silence. "What have you been up to?"

"Oh, just checkups. Then now maybe cooking. I'm sure Admiral Bardon has some things lined up for me. Just can't wait until this is all over and I can get out of here."

"So you aren't staying in the military either?" Jonathan asked. "Nik was just saying he was going to retire as well."

I figured he would. We had been gone for three years and were chased. We didn't really feel like more action —we just needed some peace and quiet. "*Ja*, ready to go sleep on some beach for a thousand years after all this."

Jonathan held up his cola. "Here, here!"

"What about you, Jonathan? Are you and your lover going to retire together? Get a little cottage and do things that would make even a girl like me blush?" I grinned.

"Oh, Rebecca, I don't think I'm capable of doing anything that would make you blush. We all heard stories from Walrum. You are one kinky *chienne*."

"You can say that again," Nik mumbled under his breath.

I laughed. For a moment it felt like old times—I felt like I was back with my friends. But reality was a cruel mistress. I took one last bite of my salad and finished it.

"I shouldn't leave the admiral waiting. See you later, Jonathan. And Nik"—I glanced at him and smiled —"*Bis Abend.*"

He nodded. "Yeah, see you tonight."

I took my tray to the dirty dishes and placed them in their correct piles. Sighing, I headed toward Bardon's office.

I pondered on what he wanted to talk to me about. It could have been about a plethora of things, including the doctor visit this morning, or it could be him wanting more information on Sebastien. I passed by cadets as they ran laps around the facility. Did I used to be that energetic? Everything that I had done for the military in the past twenty-ish years was all a blur.

Admiral Bardon's office was, of course, across the facility. By the time I got there, I would be pretty sweaty. I hoped my rose-scented body deodorant was holding up. So far I still smelled roses, so that was a good sign.

I passed more officers. I ignored their rankings and kept walking by, which probably pissed some of them off, but I really wasn't one of them any longer. I turned my back on this life the moment I was wanted for treason. No one listened to us, so I wasn't going to listen to them.

Except Bardon, of course. I would do whatever he needed of me.

I entered the building, familiar walls surrounding me. I wondered when this place had become a second home to me, and when in the world it started to feel so familiar. I went to the front desk.

"Going to go see Admiral Bardon. Here are my tags."

The ensign nodded. "Right, do you need me to lead you there?"

I shook my head. "No, I got it."

I made my way to the back of the building, trying to shy away from any other admirals. I didn't want to be formal around here anyway. I was just glad I had a higher rank than most people, if my rank was really still valid. It felt like it wasn't.

Making my way to his door, I gently knocked on it.

"*Entrez*!" Bardon called from the other side.

I opened the door and Bardon stood up. "Rebecca, I see Jonathan ran into you."

"I was actually coming this way already."

He nodded to the door. "Shut the door behind you."

I did as he asked and took a seat across from him. "So, you wanted to see me?"

He sat back down. "*Oui*. I got the doctor's report. She seems to be concerned whether the serum is going to work on you."

"Just my luck, right? I think it will though. After everything, I'm not going to let some stupid drug take me down."

He chuckled. "That's the old Rebecca I know. You never take shit from anyone. That's how you got into the military in the first place, isn't it? You were sick of taking shit from your family?"

I felt my lips twitch. "Ja. Speaking of which, I don't

ever think I thanked you for that day. You could have given me back to my parents. Actually, I'm pretty sure legally you were supposed to, but you were able to make them leave. *Danke*."

Bardon smiled softly. "You are most welcome. I can always tell when a person is in need of help. That is what got me in this career. Speaking of which..." He leaned forward, his elbows on his desk. "Why did you refuse therapy when the doctor suggested it?"

I stared at him. "You know why. So much had happened—I don't think I am ready to talk to anyone, nor do I think I want to. They might..."

"Turn you in? They won't—not if I order them not to. Nothing you say would be reported."

I laughed. "You say that, but I don't think that is true. Bardon, I don't think you realize how deeply rooted Sebastien is. He has people everywhere, and while there are many who want to take him down, there are many more who are too afraid to do so."

"Then help me find those who will actually testify against him. Do you have any?"

"That won't be taken down with him?" I raised an eyebrow. "Like I would be."

He sighed. "Then find me someone bad who deserves

to go to jail, and I can get him to testify with the promise of a pardon."

"It's been years. Most of them are probably dead."

"Well, get me a list, and I'll look into it. Can you do that?"

I nodded. "*Ja*, I can."

"*Bon*. Now, as for your testimony…"

"You promised me that if I helped you take down Sebastien—lead him to one of his facilities—that I would be cleared of everything and didn't have to testify."

He licked his lips. "*Oui*, I did, but I figured at least one of them we found there would testify against him. So far they all say they don't know Sebastien."

I started laughing. "Now you see why this was a waste of time. He has people everywhere, Bardon. Why do you think my testimony would make a difference?"

"Make the list, and if all of them are dead or missing, we will come back to this discussion. But if you do testify, I promise you won't be arrested—that is, if the information comes from you and not someone else. If someone else finds that information on their own, I can't guarantee anything. *Vous comprenez*?"

I nodded. "Yes, sir."

"Good. Is there anything else you have for me?"

I remembered why I originally wanted to come talk to him. "I was wondering if I could have access to a kitchen. The food here, well, sucks."

"Right. You don't eat meat, do you? Even though it is, in fact, vegan."

I rolled my eyes. "You sound like everyone else."

"Is there a reason you are so afraid to hurt an animal? Is that, you believe, your only redeeming quality."

Glaring at him, I went on. "Just answer the question."

"*Oui*, I can get you a kitchen. Come back here tomorrow, and I'll give you some keys. Anything else?"

I shook my head.

"Then we are done here. Now, go think about what you are going to do, and come back after you make that list."

CHAPTER SIX

Nik

I took a deep breath and let it out slowly. This was not the time to panic—I was only going out to dinner with my best friend for goodness' sake. The best friend that I'd had amazing sex with randomly for the past three years, and now her fiancé whom we thought was dead is alive. No biggie.

So many emotions ran through my body I didn't know if I wanted to scream or throw up more. I couldn't back out now, so I finally knocked on Becca's door.

"Just a minute!" she called from the other side of the door.

I rubbed my face, trying to snap out of it all. Her voice was just the most precious thing to me ever, and I wanted to hear it every day for the rest of my life.

She opened the door and was wearing what she typically wore—a tank top and cargo pants. That made me smile a bit. She really wasn't like most girls, although part of that could be due to the scars she had on her body. The other was probably the fact that those were the only clothes she had here, and she hadn't gone out shopping.

"Ready?" she asked with a smile.

I nodded. "Yup. Have any place in mind?"

We started walking down the hallway. "*Ja*, there's this little Italian place near here. They don't use eggs in their pasta."

I chuckled. "All right, pasta sounds good to me. Lead the way."

"It's a little expensive though," she began as she reached in her pocket. "But that's okay, because I swiped Jonathan's wallet earlier today."

I pinched the bridge of my nose. "How in the world

did you do that?"

"He left it in Admiral Bardon's office. I just couldn't resist."

"Does the admiral know you did that?"

She shook her head. "*Nein*, he was already back to his paperwork. I'll return it. Eventually."

"You are such a brat, you know that right?"

She stuck her tongue out at me as we stepped outside. Since it was still summer, the sun was still shining low in the sky. It wouldn't set for another two or three hours. Regenswelt was one of the few planets in all the nations to have similar day lengths as Earth. All the other planets got confusing on their days and nights. I was just glad we were on this planet so I didn't have to worry about calculating it, since it wasn't too far off from the twenty-four-hour cycle.

I peered at the familiar skyline. Even after all these years, it hadn't changed much, mainly because the downtown was as compacted as it could get. The sky was blue with clouds here and there. It would probably rain again soon, as it always did. The planet didn't get its name for nothing. If we made our way further into the city, it would be difficult to see the sky at all as the tower loomed over its people. I did not like being downtown and was glad the military base was on the edge of the city. Seeing the sky every day was a blessing.

"So," I began, not liking the silence that was coming between us. "What did you and Bardon talk about?"

She shrugged. "Just catching up and seeing what I was up to. I don't really have much going on since I'm not trusted."

I frowned. That was true—no one trusted her. Only Bardon, Jonathan, and I were given all the information. "You know it's nothing personal, right? I don't really understand why they don't give you all the information since you were the one who was able to corner him."

She held up her hand. "I really don't care. I don't want any more part of this anyway, so I'd rather be out of the loop. Once this is over, I'm out of here."

He nodded. "Right. So, where are you going to go?"

"*Ich weiß nicht*. This is one of my favorite worlds, but I feel I might be a bit safer somewhere else. Well, maybe. We did make a lot of enemies throughout the worlds, didn't we?"

I scratched the back of my head. "*Ja*, we really did, didn't we? That's going to make traveling a little harder."

"What about you?" She glanced up at me with her grayish-blue eyes. "Are you staying, or are you leaving here?"

"Um, I'm not sure." That was a lie—I wanted to go with her. "I guess it just depends on what happens in the next few weeks."

She turned forward. "*Ja*, I guess you are right."

I saw a flicker of sadness move across her face. Was that because I didn't offer to go with her? Or was it something else?

Becca changed the subject. "I can't wait to eat some real food though. It has been so long."

I laughed. "Why didn't you just go out earlier? It's not like you are in prison or anything."

"I guess it didn't occur to me. I was used to eating what I was given. I also forgot Bardon gave us money to live on, and I don't really have any other expenses."

"But you still swiped Jonathan's wallet…"

"Well *ja*. I mean, why not?"

We both chuckled. I missed being here like this. "Why don't you get yourself some new clothes? You haven't been able to buy anything for yourself for quite some time, have you?"

She shrugged. "I suppose. But if you are saying you

are sick of seeing me wear the same clothes, you know you have been wearing the same things too, right?"

"Touché. I suppose I could change up my look as well. What do you think? Should I get a suit? Or should I get some graphic tees that have weird slogans on them?"

"Just get whatever you feel comfortable in. I mean, you look good in what you are wearing now. Or maybe I'm just used to it."

More awkward silence as we stepped out of the base, giving our IDs to the guard so he could take note. He marked us down on his tablet and gave them back. Once we were cleared, we headed out onto the streets of New Dusseldorf. Since it was after work, there were a lot of people moving around the streets. I could hear a plethora of different languages spoken. Although I knew German and English and some French from Jonathan, I had no idea what a good portion of the words that were being said around us, not that it mattered since I wasn't trying to eavesdrop.

Becca, on the other hand, could probably speak all those languages. She was fluent in English, German, French, Spanish, Russian, Chinese, and Japanese, which came in handy when we were on the run and working with underground merchants. They would try to get away with stuff right in front of us, only to find out she understood everything they'd said. The look on their faces was always so priceless.

I wished I had a knack for languages like her, but I also didn't care for sitting down and studying. Our admiral, Sebastien, had forced her to learn them all, but she didn't complain. I never understood why he didn't force us as well and figured it was because she was younger, and he wanted to train her a bit different than us.

Unless it really had to do with all the illegal activity he had done, like Bardon had commented. But that couldn't be possible—we fought alongside her. We would have known. Walrum would have known.

"The restaurant isn't too far from here." Becca killed the silence. She must have noticed I was deep in thought. "Hopefully it's not too busy."

I nodded. "*Ja*, but we can wait as long as it's under an hour."

"*Ja*, I wouldn't even wait more than thirty minutes. I'm starving."

Most of the buildings in this area were about three or four stories, as we were on the outskirts of the downtown, which held the massive skyscrapers that seemed to go on forever. If I had to guess, I would say there were at least twenty square miles of buildings that seemed as if they could reach the spaceport. I didn't like being that crowded with people—mainly because I was used to being alone in a spaceship with one other person. Sure, it was a small space, but there weren't people crammed everywhere.

"Well, here it is." Becca took me out of my focus on the skyscrapers.

I turned to find we were standing in front of an almost run-down-looking restaurant, which gave it a quaint appearance. We stepped inside to find it had that old, rustic feel with wine-colored walls, low lighting, and small tables scattered around. A waiter stepped up to us before I could even take it all in.

"A table for two?" he asked. His black hair was slicked back, and he wore the classic white shirt and black slacks uniform one would see in old movies.

Becca nodded. "Yup."

"Right this way."

We followed him to a table that was near one of the walls. The waiter pulled out Becca's seat, and I took my own across from her.

"I'll get you some water and focaccia bread. I'll be right back."

"Can you even have that bread?" I raised an eyebrow as I picked up my menu. "Doesn't bread have eggs or whatever?"

"For your information, certain breads do not have eggs, and focaccia is one of them." She smiled as she looked at her own menu. "And since this place doesn't use eggs in their pasta, I get to figure out which sauce doesn't have cheese."

"You are so strange."

"But that's why you love me," she said and immediately turned red. "Or, I mean…"

"I do love you for that," I said straightforwardly. "And many other reasons."

Her face got even redder. Before she could respond, the waiter came back with the bread and water.

"Would you two like anything to drink?"

"Should we get a bottle of wine?" I asked. "I mean, it is an Italian restaurant after all."

She shook her head. "The doctor said I can't have alcohol for a couple of weeks. Something about something. Can I get a blackberry Italian soda with cream?"

The man nodded, then turned to me. "And you, sir?"

I wasn't expecting that. "Uh, I'll have the same I guess."

He went off to get our drinks. Becca peered up at me. "You didn't have to get the same as me."

"It's no fun drinking alone. Why does the doctor want you to stay away from alcohol? Is it serious?"

"*Nein*, nothing serious. Just some lady issues that are affected by alcohol. Should be fine in a couple of weeks."

That sounded like a lie, but I didn't want to be that guy, so I let it go. I glanced back at the menu. "The lasagna sure sounds good here. Cheese, eggplant, and beef? Spectacular."

She scruntched her nose. "*Wie du willst.*"

"You are, like, one of five people in the universe that is still vegan, you know that right? Like, out of billions upon billions."

Becca grinned. "It makes me unique!"

I rolled my good eye and repeated the phrase she had said moments ago. "*Wie du willst.*"

"When it comes down to it, I just don't trust the government to do their job. I mean, we work for them, or did. You know how it was. A lot of shit happens under their nose. Including Sebastien and all that he did. I mean, it had to be over twenty years now, probably more that he was getting away with shit. And still is, according to Bardon."

I glanced around. Although I doubted people were really listening in, I couldn't help but worry. "We shouldn't talk about that here."

"Right. *Entschuldigung*. I'm just frustrated."

"We all are. I guarantee that. But don't worry, it will work out in the end."

She slowly nodded. "Right."

She didn't seem convinced, but I couldn't push that here in case someone was listening in. I hadn't noticed anyone follow us here, but I also wasn't in my prime anymore. And I had been a little distracted.

The waiter came with our drinks and took our orders. I ordered the lasagna, and Becca ordered some kind of capellini pasta. We pulled apart the bread and dipped it in olive oil and vinegar as we waited. I had to admit, it was the best-tasting bread I'd had in years.

"Remind me why we are eating in the cafeteria all the time again."

She laughed. "Because it's free and convenient. But we should definitely do dinner again. It was just the two of us for so long that I took it for granted. Now it just feels weird."

"I agree. I've missed you."

"I've missed you too. Everything just got complicated so fast, which is saying a lot since, like, it was all already so complicated."

"You can say that again. But it's nice not being a wanted criminal anymore."

"Well, in this nation. I'm pretty sure we might be wanted in other regions… But at least they don't have our real names."

"That is very true. We will have to wait awhile before we travel out of here again."

I realized I had said we. Was there a *we*? Or were we just going to part ways after all this? I knew I didn't want to, but I still didn't know her plans.

Reaching across the table, I grabbed her hands. "You know I'll always be here for you, right? I… I don't want our relationship to end. You are my best friend, Becca. I just… I just wish…"

"We could have gone around acting like pirates for the rest of our lives?" She hid away the tear I saw escape her eye with a laugh. "Always looking over our shoulder and worrying we will get caught?"

"Well, not exactly. I think this mission was important and we got to clear our names. But I wish we were able to just keep on traveling after. And if you want to, I'm willing to go wherever you want."

Becca didn't answer but stared down at the bread. I waited a bit, but it didn't appear she wanted to answer.

"Or not," I said. "I understand if not, with everything that happened."

She whispered. "I just don't know what the right move is anymore. I'm sorry. Just… give me some time. Let's see how the next month plays out."

The waiter brought our food over, and I was thankful we were able to change topics due to the disruption. The lasagna was good, but I just couldn't quite enjoy it like I wanted.

CHAPTER SEVEN

Rebecca

We finished up dinner and even had some dessert. I devoured my sorbet, and Nik said his cheesecake was spectacular. The sun was beginning to set as we headed back toward the base. The street was crowded, and I stayed close to him.

"When did you stop eating meat? I remember earlier when you first joined us you weren't picky on what you ate. What changed?" Nik asked.

I was surprised he had never asked that before, and I

was thankful since I really didn't have an answer—or at least not one I wanted to admit.

"It was after I saw that documentary about how there were cases of places substituting animal products and all those sad animal eyes. I couldn't stomach it. Still can't." I turned to him with a smile. "I can show you the documentary if you want."

He shook his head. "*Nein, danke*. I still like to believe most of what I eat isn't animal. I highly doubt much is, given how big the worlds are."

"But there is still a chance. I can't help but feel sorry for them. They didn't choose their life."

"Just like humans."

I nodded. "Exactly. Never did I imagine when I was little this would be my life, but here I am. Alive. Somehow."

He laughed. "I'm surprised we are alive. There were a lot of close calls."

More than he could ever realize. "But enough morbid talk. Where should we go next for dinner? Do you know of any good places?"

"Hmm, let me think on that."

"Sounds good, just let me know when and where. I have nothing better to do."

"Did the admiral give you a place where you could cook?"

I nodded. "Yup. I am supposed to get the keys tomorrow."

"How about tomorrow you make something and we eat together? We could even invite Bardon and Jonathan. Pay him back for using his credit."

I sighed. "I suppose we could. Since he did pay for a pretty nice meal."

"Speaking of which…" He reached in my pocket and took the wallet. "I am going to return this to him before you use any more."

"Ahhh you are no fun!"

"*Was immer*. He hasn't done anything wrong. The reason you hated him isn't true. You should stop picking on him."

I frowned. I had always said I couldn't forgive him for being a spy, as that was what led Walrum to his death, but that wasn't really why I didn't like him. I didn't like him because he knew the truth about me—he knew I used to do Sebastien's dirty work.

"*Ja*. But I always did tease him before everything that happened. I can't help it, he's just so easy to be a shit to. It's that suave, ladies'-man persona—I just can't help myself."

"*Ja*, it really threw me off when I found out he and Bardon were a couple."

"I always knew, actually. So it didn't surprise me."

Nik glanced down at me. "You did? Why didn't you say anything?"

"Because it was apparent they were keeping it a secret. Besides, I figured I could blackmail him with it if need be."

"That's fair. But it's just so weird. He was always like a father to us. It's just… I don't like thinking about it. But they are happy, and I'm happy for them."

"That they are."

I had to admit, I was a bit jealous. I had always seen glances of the way they looked at each other. It was pure love—not some sadistic or masochistic relationship filled with lies. And I didn't think I could ever find someone like that. Then Walrum came into the picture, but there wasn't one second did I ever believe I deserved him.

Then there was Nik.

The air was a bit cool now that the sun was setting, and I rubbed my arms a little.

Nik wrapped his arm around me. "I should have

brought a jacket. Sorry about that."

I shook my head. "Nah, I should have brought my own. *Was immer.* I am used to the cold. And hot. And rainy. And anything, really."

"After all our missions, I completely agree. And yet you still hate the cold, don't you?"

"*Ja,* I suppose I do. But this isn't too bad." It meant his arms round me more than the temperature, but I didn't want to clarify.

We made it to the entrance of the base and gave them our ID cards. They scanned us in and we entered.

The base was quiet now. It seemed all the cadets were either at dinner or were already back in their dorms. Cadets had their own dorms, which housed a few in each room, whereas captains and officers who were visiting had a whole different wing with their own private room and bathroom, thank goodness. I didn't think I could share a room with a bunch of people again. Even if they were well behaved.

"I can't wait to get out of here. Being on base is bringing back strange memories."

Nik nodded. "That it is. I was just thinking earlier that it feels like I am at home, and yet at the same time, it doesn't. It's like a place that I just can't be back to."

"*Ja*, that's a good way to put it. Everything feels off, and I'm like a stranger somewhere that used to be familiar to me. I just want to go hide in my old ship." I rubbed my eyes as if I were crying. "But someone forced me to sell it."

"I'm sorry. We can get a new ship if you want."

There it was again. He was acting as if we were going to run off together. I knew that wouldn't be possible, not after what would happen in the next few weeks.

We made it across the rest of the base to the wing my room was in. If I wasn't mistaken, he was in the west wing, but he still took me to my door. I scanned the lock with my ID card and turned to him.

"Would you like to come in? I can offer you… well, nothing because I don't have a kitchen."

"Uh, sure."

It was awkward, especially since I didn't think he would come in. There was nothing spectacular about my room, as it was like any other apartment. Without a kitchen.

"So, uh, what's your plans tomorrow?" I asked as he took a seat on the couch. I sat on the bed.

He shrugged. "Same ol', same ol'. You?"

I nodded. "Same. Just waiting to be released."

"Right."

Normally, after an evening together like this, although never that fancy, we would have a night of some amazing sex, but part of me felt as if that would be wrong. But my heart was racing seeing him in there. I mean, why else would he have come in? The only problem was, he was acting a bit awkward about it.

I had nothing to lose, honestly. My heart was still in shambles; it's not like making the wrong move with Nik would really make it any worse. I got up and placed both knees on either side of him. I grabbed him by the back of the head and kissed him on the lips. He wrapped his arms around me and pulled me closer.

Nik, currently, was the only thing that mattered to me. I knew my heart was lying when it said that he didn't matter—he mattered more than anything, and that was the biggest problem of all. I couldn't let Sebastien know what he meant to me. I didn't want Nik to get hurt.

But I wanted him right then and there—I wanted the past few weeks to just disappear. I wanted everything to just disappear and that somehow Nik and I found each other another way. But that wasn't possible, and we had to live the lives we were in now.

After a couple of minutes of kissing, he backed away. "I can't do this."

"What?"

He shook his head. "I can't do this with Walrum alive. I can't pretend this is just a fling when I love you. And I can't go behind his back if he remembers and then you decide to go with him. I just… I just can't."

I got off of him and nodded. "All right."

"I'm sorry." With that, he got up and left me standing there. I wanted more than anything to be able to take a shot of my morphine right about then.

"I'll be back in about fifteen minutes," the doctor said after she took my blood. I nodded, and she left me sitting there.

I didn't particularly want to be on my own—not after what had happened last night. I felt horrible for Nik. I didn't want to string him along like I had been, but everything was too complex to explain. It wasn't Walrum that had been holding me back—it wasn't ever Walrum. I had loved him, yes, but I loved Nik as well.

It was Sebastien and what he did to me. What he made me do. And what he was going to make me do.

I pushed back the tears, knowing I couldn't let the doctor see them or else she would make me talk to someone whether I wanted to or not. I stood up and examined the space scenery photo, wondering if I had ever been in that exact spot.

It was just a lot of dots and a nebula—a nebula I didn't recognize. There were a lot of them out there, and I didn't have them memorized. It was always on my to-do list, but so was memorizing the layout of every major city in all the worlds. That was a lot of worlds, and I only had so much space in my brain.

Besides, what did it matter? It wasn't like I would have to ID a nebula. City layouts came in handy. Usually I didn't have to fly a ship—at least not on my own. One wasn't supposed to anyway. It was too risky that something bad would happen.

I shouldn't have been such a successful student, then perhaps Sebastien would have never taken notice of me. If I were just average, he would have paid me no regard. Or perhaps I should have never thrown that drink in his face. Then he would have never made it his mission to make my life a living hell.

Shaking my head, I tried to calm myself down. For ten years he slowly manipulated me. How did he have such patience? If I hadn't gone to surprise him that night and found him with some other girl, I would have just kept on going with him. It wasn't until then that I really understood what he had done. He had destroyed my life, my conscious, and everything I stood for.

Then he became even scarier.

The door opened, taking me out of my trance. I took a seat and listened to what the doctor had to tell me.

"So, your body is slowly adjusting. I haven't ever given anyone another dose of the serum, but I have been talking to colleagues who have, and their protocol is to wait three days, so I am going to just run tests until then, and then we can go from there. So you haven't had any side effects?"

I shook my head. "Just the sore arm but haven't had cravings or a need to grab the drug." But even without the serum, I had gone this long without the drug before.

She nodded. "Good, it seems to be working. Check in again tonight so we know you are fine, and I'll see you tomorrow."

I stood up. "*Danke.*"

"Oh, and Admiral Bardon wanted me to remind you to take another look at the list he gave me to give you. You really should talk to someone. I think that will help you through all this."

He needed to stop meddling. I smiled. "Right. I'll think about it."

With that, I left the doctor's office. As if someone could help me get through all the torture that man had delivered.

CHAPTER EIGHT

Nik

"You sure she wants us to come with?" Jonathan asked as we made our way to the kitchen area that Becca was using to cook a meal.

"Well, we had dinner on your dime last night. I figured this was the least she could do."

"I can't believe she swiped it from Jacques's office." Jonathan shook his head. "She has some nerve."

"And you have some nerve for leaving it in my office." Bardon gave his lover a look. "I told you to stop leaving your things in there."

Jonathan gave Bardon his best pouty face. "I'm sorry, I just like marking my territory."

"With your credit card?"

Jonathan laughed. "I'll admit, it wasn't my smartest move. But I also just accidentally forgot it."

Bardon ruffled the top of Jonathan's head. "You are such a *sot*."

I smiled as I watched them lovingly bicker. Becca and I were the same way, but now things were off— especially after last night. I told her we didn't have to do dinner, but she said it was fine. I hoped she was telling the truth.

Before we even approached the door, I could smell whatever she was making. I detected Italian herbs, onions, garlic. My stomach grumbled in delight. Even though I didn't have the same diet as Becca, I always loved the meals she prepared for us.

We opened the door to find her placing a casserole dish into the oven. She glanced back at us and smiled.

"Almost done! Just putting it in the oven for a little crispness."

"Thank you for cooking, Rebecca. It will be a delight tasting your food. I never knew you were a chef until

Jonathan said something."

Becca gave Jonathan a look. "And he forced me to be the chef on the ship."

He laughed. "That I did. It was fun. You know, once you leave us, you should open up a restaurant. Although people might complain about your food choices."

She gestured at the table to take a seat. "There are plenty of restaurants that have similar menus. But I don't think I would enjoy cooking for a lot of people. It ruins the fun."

"That's fair," I commented. "Just a few people makes it more intimate, but as a job it wouldn't have that special feeling."

She nodded as she sat down next to me. "*Ja,* something like that."

"So tell me," Bardon began, "where did you learn to cook?"

"At the academy, actually," she explained. "It was one of the few electives we'd been offered, and it made sense to me to be able to cook for myself in the military. I'm surprised you didn't see that in my records."

"I supposed I did. I just wouldn't think you would keep it up nor that you would be this good."

"You haven't even tried anything yet."

"*Non,* but just hearing what Jonathan had to say about your meals on the ship, I can gather you are rather good, especially since he is such a picky eater."

"Hey!" Jonathan interrupted us. "I take offense to that! I am just cultured and don't eat trash."

I shook my head. "You do realize we are in the military, right? All we eat is trash every day."

"You can say that again." Jonathan sighed. "Only Rebecca can cook a meal to my cultured taste buds. Even if there isn't any meat."

She rolled her eyes as she got up to check on whatever she was making. "Looks like it is ready."

Pulling out the dish, I saw that it was something covered in mashed potatoes. If I had to guess, it was vegan shepherd's pie—so she substituted lentils for the meat. I had it a few times before, and I had to admit, it was rather tasty.

Becca cut up pieces of the pie and dished it out for everyone. After placing a plate in front of all the guests, she also sat down.

"Thank you for the meal," Bardon said as he snapped open his napkin with a flick of his wrist. "It smells *délicieux.*"

"*Danke.* I hope you enjoy it."

I took a bite, and it was just as amazing as I had remembered. She was able to combine all the right seasonings, get the lentils to the right firmness, and have just the right amount of savory sauce. I could eat Becca's food until the end of time.

"This is amazing, Rebecca, well done," Bardon praised.

I smiled a little as I saw her blush. She wasn't used to cooking for people, and it seemed after making meals for all the crew on the ship, she was getting used to it. Bardon took another bite, his eyes flickering to her. "Next time you should add some mushrooms. I think it would give it a meatier texture."

Becca seemed like she had seen a ghost. She blinked and was back to normal. "I actually really hate mushrooms. It's the only thing I can't stand, besides meat of course."

"Right, Jonathan mentioned that. It's just interesting that you hate it so much when I believed it was Sebastien's favorite food. Or perhaps I am mistaken."

She shook her head. "*Nein,* you are correct. It is his favorite."

I had completely forgotten that. We didn't eat often

together, but the few times I had, now I recalled he usually ordered something with mushrooms.

"So perhaps you just hate it since he loves it."

"I just don't like the texture or taste. Sorry to disappoint."

There was silence. I coughed. "Well, it's delicious as always. This is one of my favorite dishes of yours, Becca. I absolutely love it."

She kept her face on Bardon for a moment longer, then turned to me. "*Danke*. I'm glad you love it."

We finished dinner, and Jonathan and I began to offer to help with dishes when she shook her head. "*Nein*, I got it."

Becca quickly got up and went to the sink to wash the dishes. Just as she stepped up to the sink, she dropped the plates and collapsed. I quickly got up and ran to her.

"Becca, what happened."

She clutched her chest. "I feel off. My chest is hurting, and I feel dizzy."

I turned to Jonathan. "Call a paramedic!"

I stayed with her and noticed her hands were shaking. She was whispering to herself, "Shit. Shit. Shit. Shit."

Now that I had a better look at her, she was sweating.

I had noticed earlier, but I figured it was because it was still hot out and she had been working in the kitchen. But now it almost appeared as if she had the flu or something. She was breathing heavily.

"Becca, what's going on?"

She shook her head. "I…"

"Morphine withdrawal," Bardon said as he stepped up to us. I peered up at him, confused.

"What?"

"She's been taking morphine for over three years and began treatment to get off of it. The side effects are starting to hit her."

I turned back to her, but she didn't meet my eye. I had been with her all that time. How would I have never noticed?

"That's impossible. Becca, that can't be true."

She didn't answer, and the paramedics came in and I moved out of the way as they examined her. I stepped over to Jonathan and Bardon.

"You can't be serious. I was with her all that time. I would have known."

"I looked over her medical records before you all went into hiding. She was prescribed morphine-B and was never given the serum to go off of it. I confronted her about this, and she said she never went to a doctor for fear they would ID you. Same for your eye. So she was going through treatment this week. Seems it isn't enough, and she's starting to detox the normal way," Bardon explained.

I couldn't believe what I was hearing. How could she have kept that from me for so long? Why didn't she tell me the truth? We could have done something even if it was on the black market. Then again, we could have done something for my eye, but I hadn't done anything until now. That was a little different, however.

Unless she didn't want to get off of it.

That was a possibility. But if that were the case, what would she want it for?

I sat in the waiting area, knees bouncing as I tried to think back on the past three years. How careful did she have to be for me to have never detect something off? She would have had to use some of our money to buy the drug as well. How had I not noticed that? How had I not seen she was addicted to some drug?

And if she was that good at hiding things, what else was she really hiding from me?

I didn't want to think about that. First I needed to be

there for her. It was the least I could do. I understood that she couldn't tell me the truth, whether it be because she wanted to stay on it or if she felt ashamed of not getting off of it earlier. Either way, I didn't judge her. I was just worried.

Some time went by before the doctor stepped out of the room and saw me. "Oh, are you a friend of Rebecca's?"

I stood up and nodded. "*Ja*, I am."

"Well, I can't give you her medical information, but you can go talk to her. And if she trusts you, get her to agree to Bardon's request to talk to a therapist."

"Sure," I said, not sure why she would refuse it nor why Bardon was pushing it. "I'll talk to her."

The doctor led me down the hallway and into a room. Becca was sitting up in a bed, a piece of machinery wrapped around her wrist, getting all her vitals.

"I'll be down the hall if you need me," the doctor said and then closed the door.

I turned to Becca. She appeared better than she had earlier, but she was looking away from me. I sighed as I took a seat next to the bed.

"Becca... *ach du liebe...* Why didn't you tell me earlier?"

"Why should I have? It wasn't your burden to bear."

"Are you kidding me? I'm your friend! I would have helped you in whatever way I could."

She finally faced me, her eyes red with tears. "Because you don't get it, all right? It was the only way I could cope. I just wanted to be able to sleep at night. I just wanted an escape always there if I needed it."

"An escape from what?"

Becca let out a sigh. "From everything, Nik. From my fiancé being killed, from us being set up, from having to serve that sociopathic admiral. I just…" She shook her head. "I started to rely on it, and before I knew it, I was addicted."

That made sense, but it was still eating at me. "You know I wouldn't have judged you."

"I know. I just… I didn't want to face it, and I felt like a burden. I'm sorry."

I placed my hand on her cheek and kissed her on the forehead. "Please, just promise me you won't keep any more secrets from me."

Her lip quivered, then turned into a soft smile. "I promise. The doctor said I should be good soon and won't have to stay here overnight. She is giving me another injection, and I just have to really monitor how

I'm feeling."

"Do you want me to stay the night? I'm sure I can get a cot or something."

She shook her head. "*Nein*, I'll be fine."

So if your friend is a mess, do you just agree to what she says, or do you make sure she's fine even though you know she is going to be pissed at you? For all I knew, she could go straight back and take morphine that night.

I grabbed her hand. "I am going to stay tonight, and then you have to promise me you'll talk to someone Bardon recommended straightaway. Will you do that?"

She rolled her eyes. "Not you too. How about this? You can stay the night, and I'll talk to Bardon tomorrow. I know he's not a psychiatrist, but he understands what is going on."

I nodded. "I'll agree to that. I'll go talk to the doctor to see when you'll be discharged. Meanwhile, I'll get a cot ready and will be waiting."

"See you later then."

I turned and searched for the doctor, worry still filling my senses. Why would she have let it get this bad without telling me? What all could she be hiding? And was I fit to be her friend if I didn't even notice, let alone someone who loved her?

CHAPTER NINE

Rebecca

I couldn't sleep with Nik in the room with me. Hearing his breath every moment made me think of how much I was hiding from him and how many times I had lied to him.

My hands were no longer shaking, and I felt a lot better. Whatever the serum was, it worked wonders. But I still craved the feeling of euphoria it gave when I took it and how it made all my fears just slip away. I didn't have to think about Sebastien—I didn't have to think about anything except the feeling of being happy for once.

I still had some of the morphine left. I had told the doctor there was no more, but that was a lie. I didn't know if there would be a point where I really needed one. So far I was all right, but who knew in the future? I didn't know what Sebastien had in store for me. Not yet anyway.

Turning over, I watched as Nik's chest moved up and down slowly while he lay in the small cot. That cot could not be comfortable for someone as muscular as him, but he wouldn't complain. He was that worried about me. I smiled a little, glad to have someone who cared enough for me. Problem was, I didn't deserve it, nor did he realize what sort of risk he was really taking by being around me. I wanted to push him away. I wanted him to forget about me, but that was never going to happen. And I couldn't do that to him.

Even though I knew what Sebastien was capable of.

It was Sebastien who had set us up to take the fall for the murder of Nash Mir's ambassador. Jonathan had believed it was because Sebastien had found out about them being spies for Admiral Bardon, but I knew that wasn't the case. Sebastien had known about their spying from the beginning; that was why he hired them all—he could keep a close eye on them. No, Sebastien set us up because he found out Walrum and I were engaged, and he got jealous.

Because I was his stupid little *Puppe*.

I rolled over again and placed my arm on my forehead. What shit hand did life deal me for it all to end up like this? For three years, every moment I hid with Nik, I feared he would just be around the corner, ready to capture me and torture me until I broke. And I had been right most of the time, but I was faster than his men. For three years I learned how to outrun everything he threw at me. Then Jonathan had to come and bring us back.

And now he was right where he wanted to be.

Bardon didn't realize how crafty that devil was—he didn't realize that everything that ever happened was always part of his plan. He was like a serial killer ready for his next target. And everyone who knew anything about him feared him for that reason. You could never be free of his grasp. I had seen it myself.

I remembered that I still needed to make a list of people for Bardon. I had begun one, the names written on a piece of paper in my nightstand. Luckily I was trained to remember names in case anything happened, but after so many years, I had a feeling most of those men and women had been discarded. They weren't needed anymore, so what was the point of having someone be able to tattle on you? That was how it worked, and that was why so many people kept their mouths shut about him.

For me, it was never fear of dying. I honestly would love to die after everything that happened. No, it was fear of the torture—what he would do to me if he found out. What he would do to Nik. And it was the shame in admitting I had done terrible things for his attention—things I should have reported right away but didn't because I had loved him. I had loved a monster.

Which was why I needed the morphine.

I thought back to what the doctor had said. She warned that my problem was psychological more than physical. She asked if anything had set me off yesterday, and I didn't want to admit that it had been something. Admiral Bardon had asked about why I didn't like mushrooms. He was testing me—seeing if I would react like I had. I proved to him what he had feared, and I felt like a fool.

And now I had to go and talk to him.

I didn't want to confess all the things I had done even though I knew he had an inkling what my purpose at Sebastien's side was. He swore that he would keep me safe, but I wasn't too sure. I no longer trusted anyone. Except for Nik and yet he was the one I was keeping at arm's length.

Rolling over to turn my back on Nik, I tried to will myself to sleep, which didn't work. My hands began shaking as I took slow, deep breaths, not wanting to have another attack. She had given me the serum, so my body didn't need it. I didn't need it.

I repeated those words to myself through the night, and eventually I fell asleep.

The next morning, Nik escorted me to Bardon's office, as if he knew I was going to go hide somewhere, and truth be told I probably was going to. I didn't want to talk to him or anyone. Even the thought of it made my arms shake and heart race. But I couldn't have another episode like I had in front of Nik. My body was getting better; it was all mental. My body was fine—or, at least as fine as it could be. I was covered in scars after all.

We arrived at the building that Bardon's office was in just as Bardon and Jonathan came walking up. Jonathan waved as he usually did.

"*Mon amis!* It is early for you two to be wandering."

I couldn't look him in the eye after what had happened last night. I knew that Jonathan knew quite a bit about me, both from his snooping and from what Bardon had told him, but I still couldn't believe I had fallen like I did last night. I liked keeping up my hard exterior, and showing any weakness, although human, made me feel even more vulnerable. I did not like being vulnerable in any aspect of my life—especially since that meant someone could take me down if they needed.

"I'm just bringing Becca around to you. I know you two had some stuff you wanted to talk about," Nik explained for me.

Bardon nodded and held out his arm for me. I took it and turned to Nik. "I'll see you later then."

He nodded and started talking to Jonathan as Bardon and I went into his office. It was the same as it had been a couple days before, sans the wallet I had swiped.

"Take a seat." Bardon gestured to a chair as he sat on the other side of his desk.

I did as he asked and tapped my hand on the desk. He didn't say anything, waiting for me to begin. I had no idea where to start. We stood there in silence for what seemed like minutes. I finally shook my head.

"I can't do this. I can't give you a report on what happened."

"You need to tell someone—you need to get the things off your chest so you can move forward."

"*Nein*, you want me to talk so you have a witness."

"I won't deny you would be a great witness, but depending on what you reveal, not even I will be able to protect you. I could give you a shorter sentence—sure —but depending on the activities that were done, you'll have people after you."

I let out an ironic laugh. "As if that is any different than what I have already dealt with. But words can't even begin to describe what happened."

"Then how about this?" He leaned forward. "Start from the beginning of everything. Start with telling me what your life was like as a child."

I raised an eyebrow. "As a child? You already know —"

"*Oui*, but perhaps once you start your story, then you can get the rest out." He leaned back and gestured to me. "What did you want to be when you grew up?"

I sighed, but it was easier than starting at the disaster. "I didn't really have dreams of what I wanted to be—

just dreams of wanting to be away from home. My parents… didn't care for me. I was a daughter they never wanted. I had an older brother they cared for a lot, but when it came to me… I was more like a punching bag for their frustrations."

Bardon didn't say anything but kept on listening. I went on.

"I got pretty good at forging signatures and pickpocketing people. It was how I survived for a while since I wasn't given anything to eat at home. Then I saw a flyer for the military cadet program and how if you had a guardian's signature, you could be sent to the boarding school. I forged their signature and went. Then, as you know, they came looking for me, and you hid me from them and didn't budge about the forged signature. They finally gave up after you gave them some money and never came back."

He nodded as I continued.

"Then I just studied like mad. I didn't care for people, so I didn't make many friends. There were some professors I was close to…" I trailed off, almost revealing a secret that no one knew. "But that was about it. I had highest honors, was the best in all my classes, even cooking, but it wasn't to impress anyone—it was just because I wanted to tell myself I was worthy.

"Then graduation came… and fifteen years later here I am." I smiled at Bardon. He raised an eyebrow. I sighed. "Fine. I graduated and wanted to go into special ops. In order to do that, we had to stand in front of all the admirals and show our strengths. It was nerve-racking, but I had heard that Sebastien didn't take just anyone. I wanted to be the exception. So at the mixer, I tried talking to him to get a feeling of where he stood on new recruits and when he hit on me, hinting that if I slept with him, he would put a good word in with the other admirals. I threw my drink in his face, and then a week later, I found out that he decided to take me on."

Bardon raised an eyebrow. "You threw a drink in his face?"

I nodded. "*Jawohl*. I figured that was going to hurt my chances with any admiral. I was surprised to learn that it actually made him want me even more. Then again, he's a sociopath who has never been told no in his entire life. So perhaps he made it his mission…" I trailed off and then pinched the bridge of my nose. "Look, Bardon, I really don't want to talk about this anymore. Not today."

He examined me for a moment, then nodded. "Sure.

Baby steps. I want you here tomorrow at the same time. Meanwhile, did you come up with a list of names?"

"I did." I pulled out the piece of paper in my pocket. "This is what I got so far. If any more come to mind, I'll let you know."

He glanced over the list. "This is a pretty long list."

"*Ja*, well, I never forget a name. But I'm not sure how many are still alive. Maybe you'll get lucky."

He let out a breath. "One can only hope. Meanwhile, take it easy, go to your checkup, and come to me if you need anything or decide you want to talk. Otherwise, I'll see you tomorrow."

I stood up and nodded. "See you tomorrow."

With that, I left him to go to my checkup.

CHAPTER TEN

Nik

I twirled my cereal in the milk, frowning. I didn't feel like eating, but I knew I had to have something or else I wouldn't have much energy. Jonathan sat across from me, practically eating everything the buffet had to offer: eggs, sausage, cereal, sautéed vegetables. It was all there.

"What's up?" Jonathan asked as he stuffed his face.

I shrugged. "I just… I can't believe she was hiding all that from me. I was with her on a ship, just the two of us, and I hadn't noticed a thing."

Jonathan nodded. "*Oui*. She is good at hiding things."

I gave him a look. "What's that supposed to mean?"

He shrugged. "She's just always so hard to read. Makes me wonder what secrets she is keeping about her life. Like, do you even know where she grew up? Or anything about her family? We know she went to the academy, but did she have friends?"

I honestly didn't know any of that information. "She also doesn't know *my* past when it comes down to it. There is stuff that I hid from her. She's always been quiet and reserved—you remember when she first was assigned to us. She kept everyone at arm's length."

"That she did and still does. I just worry whether she actually branched out a bit or if you are just letting your dick tell you otherwise."

I gave him a look. That was definitely not what was going on here. Rebecca did open up. I had seen her be weak. I wanted to protect, but there were many parts of her I just didn't know. And now with this whole morphine fiasco, I was beginning to have my doubts. I was beginning to think Jonathan's and Bardon's worries that she was involved with Sebastien's work were true.

But she couldn't have—she would have said

something—she would have confessed to me. Or she would have given evidence.

Right?

"Whatever. I think she just has been through a lot, and I want to give her space, but I also want to be there for her."

"Except now her fiancé is alive and you don't know what to do, right?"

I slowly nodded. "*Ja*, there's that. Speaking of which, have you gone and talked to him any more?"

Jonathan shook his head. "No, I was going to go after we ate. What about you?"

"Yeah, I have. Yesterday he was speaking a bit more German. He doesn't seem as angry or feral, but I don't think any of the memories have come back to him."

"Hopefully we get he snaps out of it soon and he remembers something about Sebastien that we can use."

"Hopefully. But that could take more time, and we don't exactly have time, now do we?"

"No, we don't. We need evidence by the time of the trial, which is in three weeks. I know Jacques is trying to put together a list of potential witnesses, but so far there is only Alexandra, but she was a little kid, and the court might not think that was enough. We need to find someone who had recent dealings and has proof."

I bit my lip. Who could we find? It was clear that all the people who worked at the facility we raided were working for them, but there was no proof, and none were going to confess. He had that strong of a hold on all of them. Even though we had worked for him for over a decade, I still couldn't believe he could drive that much fear in everyone from behind bars. What was the point? Why would they lie for him?

"He's a terrifying human being," Jonathan commented as if he were reading my mind. "I don't think we can even fathom what he is capable of."

After seeing what he'd done to Walrum, I knew he was right—he was a monster walking around in human skin. He had people who had his back, and those people made sure everyone else fell in line. The question was, would any of them finally confess? Or perhaps they were so wrapped in everything they feared they would be taken down with him?

Jonathan and I finished our breakfast and headed to the center where they were keeping Walrum. It crushed my soul every time I had to see him, but I really did think it was helping. I didn't wish this type of thing on my worst enemy. Well, that wasn't completely true. I wouldn't mind if Sebastien forgot all his memories and we didn't have to deal with him anymore.

No, he deserved a punishment far worse than that—he deserved to be killed.

His offense had to be severe for the judge and jury to decide to give him the death sentence. If we could prove everything he was really behind, then perhaps they would, but that was only if they could get evidence. Hopefully Bardon would find something they could go retrieve. I wasn't holding my breath though. I personally hoped he would slip up himself and confess something.

Alexandra was in the lobby as we stepped inside. She smiled when she saw the two of us. "Jonathan, Nik, glad to see you are here. I have some great news."

Jonathan and I glanced at each other and turned back to her. I asked, "What is it?"

"Walrum is starting to remember little bits here and there. He remembered his full name, which is a good sign, and that he went to the academy. I'm hoping that seeing the two of you will help trigger a little more information."

I smiled. "That's great news! Lead the way."

She nodded and led us to the room that he was

staying in. She unlocked it, and as always, I found a guard standing next to the entrance. Today he was in his bed, leaning back and staring at the ceiling as if bored. He turned as he saw us come in.

Normally when I entered, he gave me a look of confusion and distrust, but today it was different—today he had a little confusion, but then his brows moved together, as if he were trying to solve a complex puzzle.

"I… remember… you two were in my class, weren't you?"

I couldn't believe what I was hearing—he really was remembering us. "Yes, a long time ago, but yes."

Jonathan took a seat at the table. "What else do you remember at the academy?"

Walrum stood up and sat across from the two of us. "I remember… bits and pieces. I sort of remember the three of us causing trouble, doing sports… *Fußball*, if I'm correct. I did better in languages, Nik did better in math, and Jonathan… you sucked at everything."

Jonathan laughed, as did I. "Yeah, that sounds about right. And for your information, I did good in history. I can probably still kick your ass in one-to-one combat."

Walrum raised an eyebrow. "Are you willing to make

that bet? I remember getting the better of you many times at the academy."

"Do you remember anything after the academy?" I asked.

Walrum shook his head. "No, everything after that is pretty blurry. How many years ago was that?"

Jonathan sighed. "Unfortunately, *mon ami*, it was about twenty. We are getting up there in age."

Walrum nodded with sad eyes. I wasn't sure if that was because Jonathan called us all old or if it was the fact that there was still a large section of time that was still blank to him. "Right. Well, hopefully eventually I remember something. I get bits and pieces of everything, but other than that, I don't remember anything. I remember you guys, and I presume we stayed together for a while since you are here."

"Yeah, we worked together," I said.

"*Le meilleur ami!*" Jonathan patted my back. "Never left each other's sight."

Walrum smiled. "Well, I'm glad I have friends like you who have been there for me. It gives me hope that one day we can go back to normal."

Jonathan and I glanced at each other, knowing nothing would truly go back to normal, mainly because our admiral had been finally arrested. That was our mission after all—to take down Sebastien Wilde. Now that that was done, everything was up in the air.

It was true, however, that I could get my position back and start working for Admiral Bardon, but I didn't know if I wanted to do that—not when Becca might leave after all was said and done. And if he recalled everything, then he would remember her, and they might run off together, just like they'd originally planned.

At that thought, my heart sank.

I was happy that my best friend was beginning to remember his life—ecstatic really. But that also meant that I would be losing the woman I loved—the woman I knew loved me back. The problem was, she'd loved Walrum first, and I knew that was also going through her mind. I couldn't in good conscience steal my friend's lover after everything that had happened.

"You two are quiet." Walrum glanced between Jonathan and me. "There's something I'm missing, isn't there?"

Jonathan grinned. He was always the best at hiding any concern he had. "Don't worry, everything will end up fine. Just work on getting those memories back, and before you know it, we will be the disastrous trio once again."

Walrum nodded. "Right. Well, I'll be glad to join you guys once again. When that day comes. It's just so strange not knowing my own self. It's like looking at a stranger in the mirror and having déjà vu. I wouldn't want anyone else to go through what I have gone through."

And he didn't even know the half of it. Perhaps it was better he didn't remember—maybe it was better for him to think that he had simply lost his memory due to an accident and not the truth—that Sebastien had messed with his mind.

Jonathan stood up. "We better leave you to your next session with Dr. Mostovoi. We also have some things to do, but we will be back tomorrow. Just keep doing what you are doing."

Walrum smiled at us. "*Danke* for being such wonderful friends. I'm glad I have people like you helping me through this."

I tried to keep myself from confessing everything right then and there—I was not in fact a good friend. I had stolen his fiancée, and I wanted to run away with her, and part of me didn't want him to remember so then I wouldn't feel guilty about leaving with her. Jonathan placed his hand on my shoulder and led me out of the room.

"*À plus tard*, Walrum," Jonathan called over his shoulder as the guard let us out. The door shut, and I knelt down, holding my head between my legs.

"I'm a monster," I whispered as I felt tears come to my eyes.

"You're not a monster. You're just someone in love. It happens all the time."

"Stealing your best friend's fiancée after he was kidnapped by a psychopath for three years is something that happens all the time?"

"I bet it has happened at least one other time throughout history. Besides, you didn't know he was alive. I thought he was dead as well. I would never think that Walrum would stoop this low."

I heard someone come walking down the hallway. I glanced up to find Alexandra.

"What's wrong?" she asked.

Jonathan shook his head. "He feels guilty about having slept with Rebecca."

Alexandra turned red. "Oh. Right. I don't think he remembers her yet. But Nik, you thought he was dead, and we can't be sure he will care for her after all this. It's not a bad thing to love someone."

"I have loved her far longer than when we thought he was dead," I whispered. "I loved her the moment she joined our group. I just never made a move on her. I… I was about to, but Walrum beat me to it." Never did I admit that I had told Walrum how I felt before he made his own pass at her. He knew my feelings for her, but he went ahead and started dating her.

I stood back up. "Have you figured out why we thought he was dead? He didn't have a pulse?"

Alexandra shrugged. "There are many drugs out there that can make it seem like someone is dead. I presume that was what happened. Admiral Wilde had the top researchers in brain chemistry and function—there's a lot I am still not sure about, but with every passing day, we are learning more about what he did. I have gone through the charts the facility had, and it seems Walrum was the only one who was a success. They were never able to replicate it."

"Well, I suppose that's one good thing about all this." Jonathan sighed. "But even if it is just one time, that is terrifying."

"That it is," Alexandra said. "But I better go to my

next appointment. I'll see you two tomorrow?"

Both of us nodded, and she walked away. Jonathan helped me stand up.

"*Danke*," I said. "I'm glad I have you here to talk to."

"Hey." He grinned. "What are friends for?"

CHAPTER ELEVEN

Rebecca

I really had nothing to do on this base, and that made everything worse.

All that I had to keep me company were my thoughts, and that was a very, very dangerous thing. I wanted more than anything to just run, but then Bardon would come find me. If I wasn't wrong, which I rarely wasn't, he had people watching me—he probably even had people follow Nik and me the other night when we went to dinner. So running away wasn't an option. I just needed to entertain myself.

I couldn't drink, so that was out. Hanging out with Nik was a little hard and brought up things I didn't want to deal with. I didn't particularly want to cook some random things, as yesterday was still fresh in my mind. I would get back to it eventually since I was sick of tofu, but that didn't mean I wanted to rehash those memories. Which left absolutely nothing to do except work out.

The only reason I shied away from hitting the gym was dealing with other people. I didn't like working with anyone, nor did I like dealing with comments about my scars or the whispers I heard. But if I timed it right, the place should be empty due to training around the base. I would assume after lunch would be fine.

Today it was raining, like it usually was. It was a warm rain though, which was rather nice. Nothing was worse than being cold and wet. I flipped the hood on my jacket and made my way to the gym. I saw a group of cadets heading to another building, and I hoped that my assumption was correct.

As I entered, I found only one person working out— strangely, it was a familiar face. It wasn't someone I hated, so I decided it would be fine to stay. He turned, and our eyes met.

"Hey, Burt." I greeted him, not wanting to be that bitch. We had just completed a mission together after all.

He sort of waved. "Hi. How goes it?"

"Fine. Just killing time until I'm relieved. Seems you were given the chance to come back to the military."

He nodded. "I was actually never kicked out. I was just undercover."

"Fair enough. So you are one of Admiral Bardon's poor underlings."

"That I am."

We both stood there in awkward silence for a bit. I turned away from him and began to warm up before training on the other side of the gym. After about fifteen minutes, I did another ten-minute run on the treadmill.

Burt kept to himself. I could see his carrottop bouncing up and down as he was punching the large black bag in the back. I kept glancing over, curious as to how strong he actually was. I sort of wanted to find out in a hand-to-hand battle, as I only had Nik to fight for three years, except when we were actually fighting people. It was about fifty-fifty between the two of us who would win. Did they train the men here as hard as

Sebastien made us?

I went over to the weights and typed the weight I wanted them to be. After a moment, they beeped and I could pick them up. I started off pretty light—just eight pounds—as I was working more on endurance than increasing my muscle. I did not need that.

I did a few repetitions until my arms felt as if they were going to fall off. I definitely hit every muscle imaginable. After a bit, I began to work on my core and glutes. I would be feeling this all the next day— especially since it had been some time since I had used weights.

After I finished some leg workouts, I noticed a whole hour had already gone by. Burt was still working on his strikes, and I wondered how long he had been working on them before I'd come around.

I wiped the sweat off my face. "Hey, you want to fight a round?"

He gave me a look-over. "After you have worked out and are all sweaty?"

I nodded. "*Ja*, that's what we used to do while training. You never know when you'll have to fight, so always practice when you are your most tired."

He let out a laugh. "You sure about that? What if I

beat you?"

"I would like to see you try. Besides, you've been fighting with that bag this entire time—I really doubt you are at full strength." I crossed my arms. "Or are you just chicken?"

Burt raised an eyebrow. "Is the unnecessary vegan allowed to call someone chicken?"

I rolled my eyes. "Do you want to fight or not?"

He sighed. "Sure, if it will make you feel better to be defeated by me."

I grinned. He was completely underestimating me. I couldn't wait to put him in his place. This was the exact distraction I needed.

We moved to the center of the mat and faced each other. I stated the rules. "No head shots. If you raise your left hand or tap the ground three times with a hand, that means the other person needs to back off and you forfeit. Any questions?"

"Nope. Let's go."

We both held our hands up in a defensive pose. I would stay on the defensive for a bit to get a feel for his fighting style. I had a feeling it was going to be completely on the offensive side and as he moved forward. I found that I was right.

I redirected each of his strikes, trying to get him off-balance, but he was ready for that and kept his center of balance low. I had to block quite a few blows before I was able to jump back.

He grinned. "What? Was I too fast for you?"

I laughed. "*Nein*, I figured you were aggressive, but I've battled a lot of men like you—always barreling into combat. Have to admit though, you are the first to keep your balance so well."

"I didn't expect to get a compliment out of you. I'll have to tell Jonathan that his training was worth it."

"Ugh, don't tell him that. All I need is him getting cockier."

He punched again and again, but I was able to maneuver with each one or block it. I tried to get an idea of what his rhythm was, but from what I could tell, he didn't have one. It didn't matter. I understood his system.

Instead of blocking his attacks, I quickly jumped down to my hands and used my legs to sweep under his feet. His eyes were wide as he hit the ground, but he was quick to roll over so that I couldn't get on top of him very easily. He was smart, I gave him that. But he made one mistake—he told me Jonathan trained him, and I knew all Jonathan's tricks.

Before he could completely roll back up, I swung my legs, hooking them around his torso, and swung him around so that I was on top of him. I held his arms down and grinned at him.

"You surrender?"

He struggled a bit but found that I had a strong hold on him. "Fine. Whatever. I messed up a little. Let's have a rematch!"

"Did you let that *fille* get the better of you, Burt?" I heard Jonathan's voice come from the other side of the gym. I glanced up to find him standing there with his cocky grin.

I let go of Burt and stood up. "What did you expect? You trained him. When was the last time you defeated me?"

He laughed. "That's a good point, but I always went easy on you, *mon chéri*. I didn't want to hurt you."

"That sounds like you are challenging me, Jonathan."

"Maybe I am. I'm curious if you really were able to stay as fit as you claim while on the run. Let me get warmed up."

Jonathan did some active stretching as I helped Burt up. I slapped his back. "Don't worry, if it weren't me you were fighting, you probably would have won. I can show you some moves later."

Instead of some comeback, Burt nodded. "I would like that. Thank you, Captain."

I had a feeling he was keeping up a nice-guy act because his actual captain was there. He definitely didn't have anything nice to say to me when he and I were on the ship together. I found that to be quite interesting.

"Hurry up, Jonathan. I don't have all day."

"Actually, you do," he commented as he stretched some more. "You literally have nothing else to do while on the base."

I stuck my tongue out at him. "Hurry up. I'm bored."

"That's your problem, Rebecca. You are always bored. That's why you get in so much trouble."

That wasn't wrong—it was definitely one of the reasons I got in so much trouble. Although the reason I didn't like being bored was then my mind would start becoming louder, and I did not want that.

Jonathan clapped his hands. "All right. Let's do this."

The two of us went to the center of the mats. I smiled, as I couldn't wait to shut him up.

"No head shots, raise your left hand or tap the floor

three times when you want to forfeit," I restated.

"Or beg 'I'm sorry, Jonathan. You are better than me.'"

I shook my head. "You are going to be eating those words. Let's go."

We both held up our fists in a ready stance. We circled each other, waiting for one of us to make the first move. Normally Jonathan was on the offensive side, but he was waiting this time. He must have seen how prepared I was with Burt and decided to change it up, so I didn't know it was coming. I couldn't blame him for that.

Deciding to take the first move, I swung a few times at his chest, careful not to lose my balance as he deflected the strikes. I started to strike faster and faster, waiting to see what his first move would be. Unfortunately, he did exactly what I did to Burt.

Jonathan swept my feet from under me. I was half-prepared and rolled up to my hands and knees when he placed his foot on my back and pushed me down.

"*Pardon*, Rebecca. I'm not going to play nice."

He spoke too soon because I was able to turn enough where I could grab his leg and pulled him down with me. He hit the ground with a loud thud.

I quickly tried to get on top of him to put him in a headlock, but he was ready for it. He moved his head out of the way and wrapped his arm around my shoulder and rolled me over him. This was not good.

He wrapped his own thick arms around my neck and waist and flipped over into a rear hold. "Give up yet? Just say the magic words."

"As if. Groundwork is my specialty." I was able to get out as I struggled to get released from his arms and legs. There had to be a way to get out of this hold. I just had to think.

"Is that what you tell all the guys?" He laughed.

That was enough to get my blood pumping. I had to get him back for that remark. Instead of trying to move his arms, I grabbed his foot and pushed it in. He let out a groan as I knew that had to hurt his hip. He loosened his grip around my neck, and I tucked my chin and was able to slip underneath his arm. I moved his leg out of the way and grabbed his arms so he couldn't move them.

Theoretically I could strike his face right then and there, but it was against the set-in-place rules and would mean I had forfeited. What I had to do instead was flip around and move into a different hold that he wouldn't be able to get out of. Instead, I wrapped my arm around his armpits and head and pinned him down.

"Surrender now?" I laughed.

He tried to say something, but his voice was muffled by the ground and my arms.

The one thing I always forgot was how flexible Jonathan was. He was able to bring his knees all the way up and hit me straight in the stomach, which made me loosen my grip a little.

And he didn't hesitate to roll me over and pin me down just like I had with Burt.

He grinned down and smiled. "Say the magic words."

I tried to move and struggled. He did have me. "Fine. You win."

"No, say what I told you to say."

I sighed. "I'm sorry, Jonathan. You are better than me."

He got off me with his fists pumping in the air. "Yes! I did it!"

I stood up. "What's that then? Like two hundred wins for me and fifty-one wins for you?"

He pondered for a moment. "*Oui*, I think that's pretty accurate." He slapped my back. "Now go rest up. Tomorrow I think Alexandra wants you to talk to

Walrum."

I felt as if my heart had dropped into my stomach. "Is he starting to remember?"

Jonathan nodded. "*Oui*. We are hoping he will remember a little more if he sees you. That is, if you are up to it."

I more than likely wasn't, but I couldn't tell him that. "*Ja*. It will be nice to have him back."

CHAPTER TWELVE

Nik

Today was the day I'd find out if I was going to lose the person I loved.

I felt selfish thinking that. It was good that Walrum was remembering things each day, but today we were going to introduce Rebecca, and I feared that he would remember everything and want to get back together with her. I wasn't ready for that—I didn't want to lose the person I loved in a single moment.

As we walked toward the building, rain sprinkling on

us, I glanced to Rebecca. I had no idea what she was thinking. Her face was blank, as if mentally she was in some far-off, distant place. Was she happy about this? Was she thinking about all the different outcomes? Did she hope that he would remember her and she could run away with him after the trial? I didn't know.

She noticed me staring, and I blushed a little. She smiled. "I'm sorry you have been dealing with him on your own. I would have gone sooner, but I wasn't sure what would happen."

I shook my head. "No, it's not your fault. Alexandra didn't want anyone else to come yet. She wanted him to remember a little at a time."

She nodded. "Right. And so he's recalled everything up until I was with you guys?"

"*Ja*. He remembers other bits and pieces, but nothing with you."

"Does he recall anything about Sebastien?"

"Only that he was our admiral. He doesn't remember the fact that the three of us were spies for Bardon even though that happened at the academy, and he recalls most of that," I explained.

"Interesting. Maybe since it is connected to the reason his mind was wiped, it will take a while to come back."

"Perhaps. This is all out of my wheelhouse. I'd rather just beat people up and take down terrorists."

Rebecca laughed. "I agree. Or just smuggle stuff somewhere."

"I think that's technically the opposite of fighting bad guys."

She placed her finger on her chin. "You think so? It's funny that we did a one-eighty. But we never went after illegal transporting when we worked for the military. It was the least of our worries, wasn't it?"

I nodded. "*Ja*, it was."

"So," she began. "What do you want to do after this? Go back to illegal smuggling? Work for Bardon? Open some mechanic shop?"

We had discussed a little on what we wanted to do after this, but neither of us gave a straight answer. I shrugged. "I still don't know. Bardon gave us a lot for that mission, so technically I could go buy a place in the middle of nowhere and just chill for a while. But he also offered me my old position back. I'm just not sure if I want to be back. I'm getting a little old for all this *scheiße*."

"That's for sure—what, are you almost forty now?"

I gave her a look. "You didn't have to rub it in, you know."

"Oh, I know. But it's fun. Besides, if you stay in the military, you could become an admiral and deal with all the stuff Bardon deals with. Doesn't that seem like fun?"

I shook my head. "Oh hell no. I'd stay at my rank as long as I could. Then I would retire if they pressured me with more responsibilities. But what about you? Did Bardon offer you your position back?"

"*Nein*. I don't blame him. I'm a bit of a wreck. He might be waiting to see how all this plays out first or what Walrum ends up remembering."

"Right."

We were quiet the rest of the way there. I didn't want to think about all the possibilities that were presently before us—I just wanted to think back on how we'd spent the past three years together, on the run, only having each other. It wasn't the best of circumstances, as we were never safe, but I can't help to think that it was the best time I had ever had.

Except I hadn't even realized what Rebecca was going through. I had failed her as a friend and didn't deserve to be with her.

Alexandra met with us at the front of the building. The moment she saw Rebecca, her lips frowned a bit but quickly went back into a smile. She claimed she remembered Rebecca the day her parents were killed but retracted that theory as she said it was a long time ago. I wanted to believe it wasn't Rebecca, but the more I had learned about her this week, the more I learned how good she was at hiding everything.

"Rebecca, I'm glad you decided to come. I know it can't be easy for you."

Rebecca nodded. "I'm happy to help. I just hope he begins to remember everything. I can't imagine what he has been through all this time."

"We are still trying to figure that out. But that is a lot of technical stuff to try to explain. Right now we are just trying to see if he can access all his memories and perhaps tell us himself what happened. Follow me."

Alexandra turned, and we followed her toward where Walrum was still being held.

Although he wasn't being violent and almost feral, he was still under heavy guard. I wasn't sure if that was for him or to make sure that no one tried to take him— mainly Sebastien's contacts. Everything was still up in the air, and we had no idea how deep his roots were. I had a feeling, however, that they extended farther than we could even imagine.

We arrived at the door, and I watched as Rebecca took a deep breath in and out and smile. "All right. I think I am ready."

Alexandra opened the door, and we stepped inside. Walrum was on a mat on the ground, doing some sit-ups. He turned as he heard the door open, and his eyes went wide. He stood up quickly, and with every passing second, I found my heart breaking ever so slightly.

"Rebecca," he whispered. His face was sad and confused. I presumed the missing pieces were coming back to him in quick glimpses. I couldn't imagine what that felt like. I could, however, understand what it felt like for my heart to be ripped into a thousand pieces.

He stepped forward. I noticed Rebecca hesitate as he wrapped his arms around her. *"Mein Schatz."*

Yup, a thousand pieces. Completely destroyed. I tried not to run away, as I knew I needed to be there, but I wanted to so bad. So very bad.

I glanced at Rebecca's face to see if I could tell what she was thinking. Her eyes were red, but I didn't know if it was relief that her lover had remembered who she was or if it was for something else. The only reason I thought perhaps it was something else was due to the rest of her face seeming quite blank, as if she were trying to hide her emotions. Why would she need to hide them? It was perfectly natural to have a response when your loved one remembered you again.

He tilted her head to him and gave her a kiss. I peered over at Alexandra, who was still there, watching the response. She had an "I'm sorry" look on her face. I let out a small sigh.

Rebecca leaned her forehead against Walrum's and smiled at him. "How about we sit down and catch up?"

Walrum nodded as he took her hand and led her to the table. He sat down next to her, and I took the seat on the other side of the table.

Alexandra stayed at the entrance and commented, "I'll be in the other room if you need me."

Which meant she would watch on the other side of the one-way mirror. It was a little strange that all this was being watched and recorded, but it wasn't like we could ask for anything else.

"I don't even know where to start," Walrum said. It was apparent he was remembering more with every passing second.

She kissed his hand, careful not to look over at me.

"How about you start from the beginning? The others say you remember the academy and a bit after that. Do you remember when we first met?"

He scratched the scruff on his face. "I think… It was about five years after we began working for Sebastien. He hadn't added any other cadets to the team, but then you came along. You were strong and determined and one coldhearted bitch."

She smiled. "Yup, that sounds about right."

"You didn't trust anyone, and it took a while to get to know you, but we eventually did. We used to go out drinking together, although it was still rare when you would join us. You were always busy with something else."

I had never thought about it, but what could she possible have been doing all those times? Had she just been giving us the cold shoulder, or was it something larger? Did she actually have stuff she was doing that she'd never told us about? With every moment that passed, my fear that Bardon's accusations about Rebecca being correct increased.

"After about ten years into working together, the two of us got closer and started dating. Then I proposed and…" He scratched his head. "Everything is a bit fuzzy after that."

That was because he was killed or at least appeared to be killed. I wasn't sure if he had been given something to slow down his heartbeat to appear dead or if Sebastien was able to bring him back to life.

He squeezed her hand. "I just… I can't believe I didn't remember you when I first saw you."

She raised an eyebrow. "So you do remember the raid in that facility?"

"A little—bits and pieces. It's like chunks of it are still gone, and I remember being angry at everything and wanting to destroy the world. Even when I saw you, I didn't feel love but only hate. But now I remember everything."

"Don't worry. I understand. I am sorry I didn't come here earlier. We didn't want you to remember too much at one time."

He nodded. "That's what they told me earlier, but it seems that most of it is back now."

"Do you remember our mission then?" I asked.

Walrum turned to me, jumping a little as if he had forgotten I was there. "Which mission?"

"For Bardon. The one we got at the academy—the one from Bardon."

Walrum shook his head. "No. I don't remember that. I mean, memories are coming back, but things are still hazy here and there."

But he seemed to remember the years that involved Rebecca. I knew memories were strange, but the mission we had received from Bardon was our life—we had been on it for twenty-one years and counting.

"So," Walrum began. "What happens now? Do I have to stay here forever? Will we pick up where we left off?"

I watched as Rebecca tried to find words. "First you need to be back to full health. I think they are still wanting to run quite a few more tests to see what all happened. Then from there we can figure it out."

That wasn't a yes. At least I had that going for me.

"How much more time am I missing? How long was I in there?"

"Three years," she answered. "We thought you were dead. We found you before we ran away, and you had no pulse. If I had known…"

If she had known, she would have gone back for him. Our three years together would have never happened. I didn't know it was possible to feel so empty inside and yet hurt so much.

He leaned in and kissed her gently. "I know you would have come back for me. I'm sorry you had to go through all this." Walrum glanced over to me. "I'm just glad you had someone to take care of you."

Rebecca glanced around, as if looking for a reason to leave. "I have an appointment with Admiral Bardon soon, but I'll be back later."

She kissed him and stood up. I followed her as Walrum walked with us the few steps to the door.

"I look forward to it."

As we left, something hit me—how did he know I had been with Rebecca for the past three years?

CHAPTER THIRTEEN

Rebecca

He was a good actor, I would admit that, but Sebastien had given him more information than what he would have needed. There was no way that he would have known I had been with Nik for the past three years. I let out a breath as the door closed behind me. I peered over at Nik and smiled.

"Seems he is remembering everything quickly."

Nik nodded but seemed to be deep in thought. I wondered if he had noticed and this entire thing had been blown. "Yeah. We are lucky, I suppose."

He didn't say anything about what Walrum had said, which I didn't know was a good thing or not. I followed him down the hallway, feeling a bit awkward. I wasn't sure what to do with my feelings for Nik with all this going on. I wanted more than anything to run away with him, but I knew that would just end up in more misery. But Sebastien would have to find us first.

"Oh, Rebecca." Alexandra popped her head out of one of the rooms.

"Yes?"

"Can I talk to you for a moment? Without Nik?"

I didn't like the sound of that. "Yeah, but I have to meet with Bardon soon."

"It won't take long."

I turned to Nik. "See you later?"

He nodded. "Yeah, see you."

I watched as he left, and I took a deep breath and let it out slowly. This was one giant mess I did not want to deal with. Turning to Alexandra, I gave her my most believable smile.

"So, what do you need?"

She gestured to the room, and I stepped inside. Apparently it had been just her who was watching our conversation. I glanced into the room to find Walrum working out again.

"He is making a pretty good recovery, wouldn't you say?"

I nodded. "Yeah, he's a fighter. Always has been."

"Right. I'm just very surprised. From all the scans and tests I've run, I don't even understand how he's functioning. The doctors that Admiral Wilde had hired are some of the most brilliant. But they won't say a word of what they did, and they deleted all their research—or at least deleted it from what we were able to grab. I'm sure it's on a file somewhere. Otherwise, what would have been the point?"

"Who knows with Wilde. He's a little psychotic if you haven't noticed."

I watched as she hid away her fury. "That I know. I'm not sure if you heard, but my parents were scientists who studied brain chemistry."

Scheiße, did she figure it out? "I think you might have mentioned that when we were on the ship."

"Right. Well, they were both murdered by Admiral Wilde because they wouldn't help him with his mission ten years ago."

"I'm sorry for your loss. He has messed up many

lives. I hope we are able to finally send him to hell after this is all over."

She nodded. "I agree. We just need someone to provide proof."

"Do you think Walrum will be able to?"

"I'm not sure. With everything erased and none of the people we took in willing to confess they know him, I am starting to have doubts. All the tests are showing some change but not enough for where he is at. It is quite strange. I'm not sure what to make of it."

I studied her, trying to figure out where she was going with all this. "What do you mean?"

"I mean, after going through all the scans we have taken, the change in how his brain is functioning isn't that drastic from when we'd first taken him in, and yet he is acting almost completely normal, other than not remembering anything from the past three years. His brain should have changed a bit more than what I am seeing."

I shrugged. "I know nothing about science, so I'm not sure what to tell you."

She narrowed her eyes. "I think there is more going on than we realized, and I think you are holding on to information that could help us."

I let out a laugh. "You think I am hiding information that could help my fiancée? You think I like seeing him like this? I almost killed Sebastien when I found out. I wish I had, but Nik pulled me off him. I want more than anything to send that *yobannyy zasranets* to hell."

She blushed a little from my language. "If you hate him so much, then testify."

My eyes widened. She did remember. "Testify against what? I served him for over ten years, and not even I have proof. Neither did Walrum nor does Jonathan and Nik. Speaking of which, I have a meeting with Bardon. I'll stop by tomorrow to talk with Walrum some more."

I turned and headed toward the door. She grabbed my wrist.

"I know it was you that night. Admiral Bardon told me that it wasn't and to not mention it to anyone, but I remember it like it was yesterday. Your hair was a different color back then, but I know it was you. You slowly drowned my parents in front of me. You tied them up above their work sink and filled it with water. And I had to watch it all."

I stared straight in her eyes. "I don't know what you are talking about. I wasn't there."

She squeezed my wrist tighter. "Yes, you were. I saw you, and you met my eyes just as you are now."

We were both silent for a moment when she finally let go of my wrist. She tried to gather herself.

"After dealing with this mission and seeing how thick and strong his web is, I know you had your reasons for not disobeying him. I have read your medical records, and I can only imagine what he put you through."

I narrowed my eyes but didn't say anything.

"But if you have some kind of proof that could sentence him to death, please do it. For everyone who is stuck in his web."

"If you think a little proof will stop him, you are dead wrong. He's a lot craftier than we give him credit. Now, excuse me."

I turned and headed toward Bardon's office. I would need to let him know Alexandra was still fishing for information, not that she needed it. She had known it was me for a while, but as she said, Bardon told her to stay silent since all of this was a complete mess with me right in the middle.

But she was right. I could give all the evidence they needed, but if I did that, I was putting a mark on my back. There were dozens of people, who if they knew the truth, would come for my head. Then there were Sebastien's men. Then there were just general officers who would want me in prison for my crimes.

My hands and arms began shaking, and I clutched my wrist with my other arm. I had to keep everything in check. I had to keep my emotions from surfacing.

Otherwise, I was going to make a big mistake.

I made it to Admiral Bardon's building and checked in. I walked past all the officers, nodding to each of them. I wanted more than anything to be done with this life. But I knew better than to wish for things that would never happen.

I knocked on Bardon's door, and he answered from the other side. "Come in."

I entered and found that he had a few screens going as he was finalizing whatever he was working on. He turned the screens off and smiled at me.

"Glad you were able to make it today. I wasn't sure since I know you went and saw Walrum first."

I nodded. "I did. He remembered me." Or at least it appeared that way.

"And?"

"And… I don't know what you want from me. I don't know what to feel anymore. I don't know what's real and what is some kind of twisted lie because Sebastien has fucked me up so much."

"This is why I said you need to go to a therapist."

"And I told you that I am way past anyone fixing me."

"Rebecca…"

"What do you want from me? You know I'm not innocent. You have been trying your hardest for it not to be leaked for some odd reason and even told Alexandra to not worry about me and not to say anything. So I can't help but wonder, why are you trying to ignore my past? Do you see me as that innocent teenager who came to you for help? Or is it something else?"

Bardon was silent for a moment, as if trying to find the right words. "I… I can't help but feel responsible."

I let out a laugh. "Responsible? What in the world would you be responsible for? This was all Sebastien's doing. I don't know if you have noticed this, but he is an obsessive asshole."

He shook his head. "I knew he was going to hire you and that the odds were that you would get caught in the cross fire. I haven't forgiven myself for that. I should have demanded that he let me take you on. But I was too afraid."

"That you would jeopardize the mission that Nik and the others were on." I laughed harder.

"What is it?"

"He always knew you were onto him. It wouldn't have mattered either way. You realize that he knew, right? He always knew. That was why the three of them didn't find anything for so long."

Bardon's face froze. "How do you know that?"

"Because he told me to stay away from you. I knew everything. I could have come to you years ago, but I didn't. You know why?"

He didn't move because he did know why.

"Because everyone is afraid of him. Because he has his fucking claws dug into everyone's back, and there is no way you'll be able to take them out without losing lives. If it were easy to just confess, I would have done it long ago. You know that. I know that. That is why you wanted to set him up like you did. But alas, here we are with no proof."

Bardon took a moment to gather his thoughts. He knew I was right. All of this would be for nothing if we didn't find some kind of proof. Even if one person confessed—even if I confessed—it wouldn't bring him down because there would be someone on the inside, spinning it all.

"Fine. You are right. You don't need to tell me everything that happened because it isn't going to help us. I already have the names you provided. But that isn't why you are sitting here, Rebecca. You are sitting here because I actually do care about your well-being and want you to work through all the things he did to you. You understand that, right? That there are people in this world that care about you. Or has he destroyed you to the point where you aren't sure what to feel anymore?"

I frowned. He had me there. "It's not that I don't know how to feel—it's the fact I'm afraid he's going to take it all away from me again."

Bardon furrowed his brows. "*Attendre*. Rebecca, you said Sebastien knew about my men all this time. Then what was the purpose of him setting you all up?"

I opened my mouth, but nothing came out. I could feel tears rush to my eyes and fall down my cheeks.

"It was because of you, wasn't it?" he whispered. "Because you were engaged."

I nodded slowly, trying not to completely break. It was because of me that Walrum had been tortured and experimented on. It was because of me that Nik and

Jonathan had to go into hiding. It was because of me that there would never be any evidence found.

Bardon stood up and moved to me. He knelt down and wrapped his arms around me. He didn't say anything but let me sob on his nicely pressed military uniform.

CHAPTER FOURTEEN

Nik

Two days had passed since Walrum remembered Rebecca. I let them talk together alone as I didn't want to be there. I kept my distance from her since I wasn't sure what to say or discuss. It felt as if our relationship was over and that we would never get to be the friends we once had been.

During the entire time, I stuck with Jonathan, who patted me on the back every time he could tell I was thinking about it. He didn't try to give me advice, as what sort of advice would he even give? It wasn't like this was anywhere near normal.

Today, however, we were all requested to meet with Admiral Bardon in his office. I didn't expect to see Rebecca there, as usually it was just Jonathan and me being called. She was already there, taking the only seat. Jonathan leaned on the wall behind Bardon, and I leaned on the back wall behind Rebecca.

"I am glad you all could make it," Bardon began.

Rebecca crossed her arms and leaned back. "Because we have nothing else to do."

"Right, but you like to hide on the base, so there is that."

I held back a laugh as Bardon went on.

"I have acquired a list of names that are connected to Sebastien. I went through the list and found that only one is still alive. His whereabouts were a little tricky to find, but luckily for us he is on Regenswelt. I want the three of you to retrieve him and bring him back here."

That sounded simple enough. "Why us?"

"Because you three are the only ones I trust right now. I know you work well together, and you know how critical it is to get this person."

Jonathan nodded. "It makes sense to me, but maybe

Rebecca should stay here with Walrum to make sure he's fine. It seems that he's getting better each day."

"This mission won't take long, a full day tops, so I think leaving Walrum alone will be fine. He knows how things are for the military and will be patient," Bardon explained.

I couldn't see Rebecca's face, so I wasn't sure what she thought about the mission. She was unusually quiet.

"Is there any other information we need to know?" I asked.

"There is the possibility that Sebastien has this person being watched, per usual. Keep your eyes open and be quick."

Simple enough. He handed Jonathan the tablet with the information. Jonathan scanned over it, nodding his head.

"Our target is Lars Söderholm. He's forty-two years old and has been living on the outskirts of Lake Neumaschsee. It is pretty rural out there, so he's going to notice people coming up to his place."

"So we have to be quick and silent. Sounds like no problem for us," Rebecca commented as Jonathan gave her the tablet.

She skimmed the information and handed it to me. I

glanced it over. The man appeared tall, lanky, with white-blond hair and green eyes. Even in his photo he appeared like he didn't trust anyone. This was going to be fun.

Bardon continued. "I have transportation ready for you all. You can go to the prep room and pick out whatever you need. Be ready to leave in an hour."

The three of us left the room and headed toward the prep area that was full of weapons and any other gadgets we might need. With an operation like this, a handgun would definitely come in handy in case Sebastien did send some people. As we went into the room, I became almost giddy with excitement. It had been so long since we were on a mission. I missed the old days. Well, sort of.

Rebecca was quick to snatch the butterfly knife and a small TK7 gun. That didn't surprise me as it was easy to put on one's person but carried the normal round of bullets. I grabbed a Y437 pistol and a tactical knife. I also grabbed a stun gun, as I had a feeling the guy might need to be stopped if he tried to run.

Jonathan snagged a tranquilizer gun, a Y437 pistol, and at least four knives. I raised an eyebrow to him, and he shrugged.

"You never know. Besides, the two of you are used to having nothing since you had no money."

Rebecca and I glanced at each other and shrugged. He had a point. It was supposed to be an easy mission —just in and out—so there was no reason to pack huge guns.

"I never thought I would do a mission like this again." I sighed as I stretched. "I think I might be getting a little too old for it all."

"Yeah, you are." Rebecca smiled. "Meanwhile, I'm still in my prime."

Jonathan and I both gave her a look as she laughed. She was only a few years younger than us, but that didn't make much difference once you started getting into your thirties. And now Jonathan and I were almost forty. I was not looking forward to that birthday.

"So, do you think he will get us the information we need?" Rebecca asked as she leaned against the wall. Jonathan was still going through gadgets. "I mean, would one person really bring down the great Admiral Wilde?"

Jonathan threw me an earbud. He tossed one to Rebecca as well. "I think we need to grab all the people that we can. If he will help us, then it is worth it."

"And what if it is a setup? What if it is really a bunch of men ready to kill us?"

Jonathan smiled. "I would like to see them try. And if that is the case, we kill all but two, bring them in, and interrogate them individually. You know how it goes. One will snap if we make it seem the other betrayed them."

That brought back memories. I leaned on the wall across from Rebecca. "Like that one time. And that other time. And that other time."

Rebecca laughed. "Yeah, pretty much. I miss those days. It was a miracle we got anything done with all the stunts we pulled."

"We, *mon pote*? I do believe that was you and Walrum who'd caused the most trouble. If I'm not mistaken, you almost cost a representative their position one time."

"Heh. That was a long time ago, but yeah. We did."

"I can't even imagine all the trouble the two of you got into when you were on the run. Especially since we found you smuggling."

I glanced at Rebecca, and both of us had a smug grin. I licked my lips. "I'll just say, I'm glad Becca can speak a billion different languages or else we would have been screwed."

Jonathan raised an eyebrow. "Oh, do tell more."

Rebecca stepped up to Jonathan and patted his cheek. "Yeah, no. I'm not telling you diddly squat, Jonathan. You might go back and report it to your *papa*."

Jonathan turned red as I about choked on my spit. I knelt down, laughing harder than I had in a long time.

"Now." She turned to the rest of the gadgets we had available. "What else should we bring today?"

We ended up grabbing a stun grenade, a few flares in case we got separated, and cuffs. Though we had the possibility of running into Sebastien's men, we weren't going to go in, guns blazing, and scare off the target. We needed him back alive and believing we would protect him no matter the cost.

The location was about three thousand miles to the southeast, but in our helicopter jet, it would only take about two hours to get there. We would land a ways off so he didn't see us coming, which would be another thirty minutes to hike to the house. It was secluded and well hidden but not hidden enough. He must have been riding on the fact that Sebastien was protecting him from the inside, which meant he was a valuable asset.

I sat in the cabin of the 'copter with Jonathan and Rebecca, waiting until we landed, and wishing this mission was after I could take off my eyepatch. It would be fine, though, as I had gone years without it. It had been a while since I had to take someone in alive, though, other than Sebastien, but that was a bit different. We had a lot of people on that mission, and there was also the fact that I was more concerned about saving Rebecca than dealing with anyone else. This time I had to focus on one person—a person who did not want to be found.

Glancing up at Rebecca, I found that she was resting her eyes. Although I hadn't seen her much in the past couple of days, she seemed to be doing a bit better. I didn't know how she was feeling about Walrum's progress, however. Was she glad he was doing better? Did she feel complicated about it like I had? Was she going to run off with him after all this was over?

I didn't go with her to visit Walrum, but I did go later in the day with Jonathan. He seemed to be doing really well and mainly talked about Rebecca the entire time, which sucked for me and caused me to drink a bit each night. Then it didn't help I was getting older and I woke up each morning hungover. I was just glad there were pills for that now.

But he was getting better, and that was a good thing. He was starting to remember the mission that Sebastien had sabotaged. Although it was just bits and pieces, it was progress and eventually he might be helpful for us.

From what I knew, Sebastien hadn't said a word to any officer and was staying quiet. I wasn't ready to see him as I knew I would want to beat him into a pulp, which wasn't allowed. So far Bardon hadn't requested us to talk to or see him, so we were keeping our distance.

Rebecca also hadn't gone to see Sebastien nor had she been asked to. I had a feeling he was the reason she had been taking the morphine-B, so I doubt Bardon would have her talk to him anytime soon. This mission might change that though.

Jonathan checked his watch. "We are getting close. Shall we go over the plan once more?"

Rebecca opened her eyes and nodded. I did the same.

"Right, so we will be coming in from the north." He held up the tablet so we could see. "We will stick together until we get near his place. After that, we will split up so we can surround him, and he won't have any place to run as the south part has a lake."

"And what if he has a boat?" Rebecca asked. "I mean, these guys usually have a boat."

Jonathan stared at the map. "Okay, first one of us destroys the boat. Nik?"

He nodded. "Yup. Go straight to the boat. Got it."

"Good. Rebecca, you and I go in from these two angles and keep an eye out for the target."

"And for Sebastien's men," Rebecca commented. "Because let's be honest, they are there."

I agreed. "Yeah, there's no way he isn't keeping an eye on the place. The fact that everyone else has been killed makes me wonder if this isn't a setup."

We all were silent, as we knew it was true. This smelled fishy, and if we knew Sebastien, which we did, he probably had this all ready for us to get back at us for capturing him. He was devious like that.

"Well then, we just take out more of his men. It's that simple." Rebecca leaned back and closed her eyes. "It isn't the first time we have dealt with his shit, and it won't be the last. Until he is dead, we will be dealing with him. Then again, maybe even after."

She had a point. We were tied to him by then, and he wasn't going to give up without a fight. We would have to do everything we could to take him down, and perhaps after all this was over, we could finally rest.

As if that were going to happen.

CHAPTER FIFTEEN

Rebecca

Lars Söderholm. I was surprised he was still alive, because from what I remembered he was a bit slimy and not someone to trust with the secret that he had. Then again, money was his motive even though he lived all the way out here. If I had to hazard a guess, he put all his earnings into traps surrounding the building. I couldn't wait to see what he had in store for us.

But would he talk? I highly doubted it. He was afraid of Sebastien, as everyone was. But perhaps he had some paperwork or proof of Sebastien's dealings—more than likely to use as blackmail if need be.

Which was exactly why Sebastien's men were probably on their way.

It was only the three of us and Bardon who knew of this mission, but the pilot could have realized where we were going, and if he had any connections, he would have alerted Sebastien by now even if he was in prison. I didn't say anything of course, as I knew it wouldn't be needed.

And because I knew I needed to be careful what the person would reveal, as he might blackmail me as well.

I would have to check all the data first. Or if Bardon was looking it over, he would make sure I was in the clear for whatever reason. He didn't make sense, or I just wasn't used to someone like him looking out for me. He said he felt responsible, but no one except Sebastien was responsible for the things that had happened. And some of it had been my own fault.

Because I should have never believed his lies.

Pushing those thoughts behind me, I stepped out of the helicopter jet and glanced around. It was a pleasant day since we were farther south than the capital. It seemed calm all around us, but I knew that could change in an instant. I turned back to Nik and Jonathan.

"You two ready?"

They nodded, and we ventured into the woods together.

It had been a while since I had been in a forest like this. Most of Nik and my activities for smuggling were in the cities, as it was just easier to do business that way. That didn't mean there weren't some outposts in the middle of nowhere, however. We just didn't want to deal with those jobs. It was bad enough dealing with the men that we did. Any smuggler who was this far out in the middle of nowhere was paranoid, and it never ended well. I would know, as we had been on missions for the military to take down scum lords like that.

Luckily it was rather flat, and we didn't have to hike up or down a mountain. All we had to do was keep moving forward until a certain point and then split up.

The birds sang from up in the trees, and the air smelled of sweet pine and cedar trees that had been brought over during the terraforming process of this planet. Nothing beat the smell. I wished I too could live in a forest like this. Perhaps one day. Who was I kidding? I doubted I was going to make it out of all this alive.

This mission would be a cakewalk; however, it was more of what would come later that I was worried about. Sebastien wasn't going to go down without a fight, and I would know since I was part of that plan. He went over everything before Bardon and his men showed up. If I spoke of it, however, he would kill Nik. The deal was if I went along with it all, then he would spare Nik's life. Although Sebastien was a liar, he kept a promise like that.

Which meant this plan had to go smoothly.

Little squirrels scurried around in the bushes, making me jump a little each time. It was amazing how loud a squirrel could sound and seem like it was a giant monster. I took a deep breath and let it out slowly.

"Just a squirrel. Don't worry about it." Jonathan laughed.

I gave him a look. "Did it seem like I was worried?"

"A bit. Don't worry, Nik will protect you from a horrible monster like that, so you have nothing to worry about."

I glanced over at Nik. He shrugged. "I'll make sure they don't nibble on your toes."

I rolled my eyes but couldn't help but smile. I missed this—the two of us having fun like this even though

Jonathan was here. I didn't really have any problem with Jonathan; he just got on my nerves more often than not. He could always tell what I was thinking, which frightened me. I didn't like it when people were in my head, as it happened too often than not.

We kept on walking and didn't run into any traps or other men who might be out for our target. I was a little surprised, as usually we ran into trouble right away. Perhaps they knew what our strategy was and would be waiting for us to split up. If that were the case, then I needed to give them more credit—they knew what they were doing.

"We should split up here," Jonathan said as he checked his watch. "Nik, you go and destroy the boat. Rebecca, you go in from the northeast, and I'll come in from the northwest. If you run into anything, use the earbuds to alert the others. We can't let the target get away, but we also can't die either."

"No dying. Got it. Anything else?" I smirked.

"I mean it though. Be careful. We haven't run into trouble yet, but I have a feeling they will be showing their ugly heads soon."

Nik and I nodded and headed out in our respective directions. I pulled out my gun, listening closely for any movement that wasn't little animals. I didn't see anything or sense anyone, but that didn't mean there wasn't something going on.

I could see the house in the distance now. It was quaint but would be enough for one person. As we expected, there was a boat tied to a little dock. We would have to slow down to make sure Nik got to it before we set anything off.

The windows were open, which was a good sign as that meant it was likely someone was home enjoying the nice day. I didn't see any signs of him being outside. Hopefully he wasn't traveling out in the woods or something but was inside lounging or doing dishes.

And hopefully Sebastien's men hadn't already arrived and killed him.

By the looks of it, nothing seemed disturbed, but I was still a significant distance away from the house to tell. I examined around for any traps but didn't see signs of any. Was this guy that trusting? Or was I missing something?

I radioed in to the others. "Home in sight. No signs of attacks yet nor any type of traps. Anything in your sights? Over."

"No sign of anything. I am almost to the boat, but it

appears to be well maintained. Over," Nik said.

"Nothing on the northwest side. I am still making way to the house. Over." Jonathan was apparently having the same experience as we were.

I frowned. I preferred running into danger early as the suspense was always the worst. I wanted to know where my enemies were and what they were up to, otherwise it was just a guessing game, and most of the time I thought up scenarios way worse than they could ever think of. That was more than likely due to all the time I had spent with Sebastien and the things he made me do.

As we were almost upon the house, I saw Nik in the distance sabotage the boat. Now he had no quick way to retreat. I moved a bit faster to the target. I could see Jonathan on the other side.

And that was when the target bolted out of his home and ran into the woods toward where I was. I grinned, darting to the right so I could cut him off. He apparently didn't think that through as he acted as if there were no other people in the woods. He would be in for a rude awakening soon enough.

I had to admit, this guy was fast, but if you were worried about running from Sebastien or his henchmen, you would learn to run fast. I, however, had been running away for three years and made sure my legs were in good shape. He made it about a hundred and fifty meters before I tackled him to the ground. He screamed as I struggled to put the cuffs around his wrists.

"Lars Söderholm, you are under arrest for conspiring against the government."

"No!" he screamed. "You can't take me in! I was promised to be left alone if I stayed out here!"

"Well, Admiral Wilde is under arrest, and his contacts are now being questioned."

I pulled him up, and the moment he saw my face, he went white. "You! *Nej, nej, nej.* You are going to kill me! You are his right-hand man! If he's arrested, then why aren't you? No, you are going to take me somewhere and kill me! That is what you do! You killed all my men!"

I sighed. I knew this was how it was going to go. "Look, you are being taken in as a witness. I do not work for Admiral Wilde."

"Yes, you do! I remember your face! I'll tell them everything! Let me go, or I'll share your secrets as well."

That was exactly what I was telling Admiral Bardon. He'd said not to worry about it because he would talk to this witness before it all went on record.

That, however, was not what I was going to do.

Before I could figure out the best way to shut this guy up, his head went straight into mine, sending me tumbling back. I stumbled and fell right on my ass as he ran off farther into the woods. I was about to let Nik and Jonathan know that he'd gotten away and I was about to pursue him when suddenly part of his head exploded, and he fell to the ground, dead.

It was a bullet. A bullet had gone straight through him. He was gone before he even hit the dirt.

"*Scheiße.*" I pressed the button on my communicator. "Target has been killed! Other men here! Take cover!"

I bolted straight for the body and pulled him to some cover. The shot had come from the west, so I needed to keep something blocking me from that side as I searched the body. If I knew this man, which I kind of did, he would have some evidence to bargain with on his person. I searched his pockets and found a small USB.

"Bingo."

Now the snipers would be after me. I leaned around the tree to get an eye on my opponent. Bullets hit the tree, making bark explode and almost hit me in the eye.

"Fuck!"

I grabbed my gun and got it ready. I was able to pinpoint where he was in the foliage. I took a deep breath and let it out slowly. He wouldn't be the only one, but at least it would give me the chance to take cover.

Turning, I shot three bullets in the direction I knew he was in. I waited for a moment, listening for any signs of him, as I was still peeking my head around the tree. There were no sounds. I had hit my target.

Standing up, I ran as fast as I could to the house to get out of the firing range and plan what we were going to do to get out of there.

CHAPTER SIXTEEN

Nik

After Rebecca ran into the small home, we closed the door and smashed one of the windows open so Jonathan could aim outside as we discussed what to do next. So far, no bullets came raining down on us, nor did we have sights on the attackers or an idea of how many there were.

Rebecca went straight to the computers, opening up and hacking his password. "I'm in. It seems he did have some cameras around the area, which is why he bolted.

From these, I see about…" She bit her lip. "Five attackers, one of which I already killed. I wasn't sure, so I am glad I can see them on this."

"Are they moving in?" I asked as I stood over her shoulder.

"Of course. They have the place surrounded." She laughed. "Too bad we don't have a boat."

"Hey, you are the one who said that we should destroy it."

"I know. I'm just stating a fact. Anyway, Jonathan, do you have any visuals yet? There should be one coming out of the forest line to your ten o'clock."

Jonathan nodded. "Yeah, I see him." Jonathan aimed and fired. Rebecca and I watched the screen as the man went down.

I turned to Jonathan. "Nice shot."

"*Merci*. But we aren't done just yet."

"Jonathan is right… It seems more are coming."

I whipped my head back around. "What do you mean?"

She pointed to the screen. "A dozen just came within sight of this camera. We are now outnumbered fifteen to three."

"We've been outnumbered by way more," Jonathan

commented. "But we didn't exactly come prepared, now did we?"

Rebecca replied, "I have fifteen rounds left, Nik has about seventeen, and Jonathan, you should have fifteen as well right?"

"Yeah, so we just have to hit them within three shots."

"Piece of cake." Rebecca grinned. "Or we can go out there and take them out one by one with knives, which is my vote. I always love seeing their faces as they die, knowing we took them down with a knife when they have giant guns."

I patted her shoulder. "Now, now, we need to survive. Jonathan and I can take the windows, and Rebecca, you give us their locations."

"Sounds like a plan," she said as she pulled out her own gun and got it ready, just in case. "Let me know when you want to switch."

"Will do. I am also going to see if I can get any more information off this computer before they try to take a machine gun to us."

"Do any of them have a machine gun?" I asked as I smashed out my own window.

"Yup. Three of them do. They are still out a ways. I'll

keep you informed when they move closer so you can try to take them out first."

"That would be very handy, Becca."

"I know. I'm so helpful like that."

Nik smiled. It was definitely just like old times. He heard her tap the screen and keyboard, searching for what information she could find. I glanced out the window, scanning for any movement. So far, there was nothing.

"Nik, to your two o'clock," Rebecca said.

I turned my attention there and aimed at the man. I took my shot, and he hit the ground. "Sixteen to go."

"Congratulations, you know how to aim." Rebecca sighed. By the sounds of it, she was still trying to hack the computer.

"Do you really think he would be stupid enough to not erase his files?" Jonathan asked.

"I think he's stupid enough not to completely know how to erase it from the computer. There can always be traces of files if he wasn't too careful. He didn't seem to be the careful type since he tried to run for it, knowing we were here. Smart thing to do would have been to hunker down. Or make traps."

"I take it that one of these guys shot our target."

"Yup, but I found a USB on him. But I don't know what's on it, so I want to make sure there isn't more we could be missing."

At least we had something. I peered out the window and didn't see movement. "What's going on outside?"

Rebecca answered, "They are trying to surround the area. They realized we are picking them off one by one, so they are staying back for now. We are going to be in trouble soon though."

I didn't like the sound of that. That meant we would have to be face-to-face, and they would have time to set up the machine gun and destroy the building.

We hadn't been in a situation like this in a long while. I shouldn't have been so familiar and happy about it, but I couldn't help it. Adrenaline always kept me going.

"Any luck on finding things on the computer?" I asked, eyes still set on the tree line.

"Nothing yet. Perhaps he was smarter than I thought." Rebecca let out a sigh. "We will just have to hope everything is on the USB I found on him. I presume it will be, as it was probably the only thing he had to bargain with."

"As if Sebastien ever bargains," Jonathan mumbled.

"Two men coming in. One at Jonathan's eleven and one at Nik's two."

I saw movement and took a shot. The man didn't go down, so I shot another and he hit the ground. Jonathan only took one shot to hit his opponent.

"What?" Jonathan grinned. "Are you losing your touch?"

"Shut up. I've been good so far."

"Fourteen more. It doesn't seem there have been any more incoming from earlier. Remember, we have to keep two alive to interrogate later," Rebecca said. "It seems the two with machine guns are setting up, but they are a ways out, and we won't be able to shoot them with the guns that we have. Not accurately anyway."

"We have a few stun grenades and flash bombs. If one of us wants to go out there, we can definitely make a distraction and cherry-pick them," Jonathan commented.

I sighed. "*Scheiße*… Fine, I can go out there. But Becca has to keep me informed to where everyone is."

"Nah, I'm going to leave you out there to fend for yourself."

I glanced back to find her grinning. She rolled her eyes. "Of course I am going to report it all to you. Why wouldn't I?"

"Fair point." Turning back to Jonathan, I found he was already unclasping his grenades and bombs.

"Which way are you heading first?" Jonathan asked.

I glanced over to Rebecca. She answered, "One is setting up fifty meters to your 1 o'clock and the other to the 11 o'clock."

"I guess I'll go for the northeast one first. Get ready."

I covered my eye as did Rebecca, and Jonathan threw the flash grenade in front of the house. It went off, shaking the small house, and when I knew the coast was clear, I bolted to the east of the house and into the woods.

Rebecca's voice came into my ear. "Okay, there is a guy to your eleven. About ten meters."

I crept quickly, listening for the man. Whoever these attackers were, they were well trained. It wouldn't surprise me if they were part of the military and didn't know who they were actually working for. That wasn't our problem, however. Admiral Bardon would have checked all mission postings and canceled any that would interfere with our own. We had to defend ourselves.

The man had a gun at the ready as he was creeping

up to the house. I shot him in the head without a moment's hesitation.

"Good. Now there is no one between you and the guy setting up the machine gun. He's about thirty meters to your two o'clock." Rebecca was on top of searching me out.

I was surprised the target didn't try to run earlier, but perhaps he had to take time to gather what he wanted and erase everything. It was apparent, however, that those other men came in after us.

Which meant someone leaked the information.

This mission was on the down-low. It wasn't even recorded by Admiral Bardon, so how could have anyone report in so fast. It had to have been with the pilot, or there had been people watching this place all along. Either way, we were going to get our information, and we would win.

We had some evidence, even though it would have been better to have the target report everything in person. We would have to make do. The important thing for now was to make it out of there.

I could see the man setting up his machine gun. I aimed and took a shot straight at the back of his head. I pulled the trigger, and he was dead in an instant. I let out my breath and waited for Rebecca to radio back in.

"Clean hit. Now the other sniper is about two hundred yards to your five o'clock. But there are also about…" She mumbled to herself, counting. "Seven individuals between you and them. How many more bullets do you have?"

I did some math. "Twelve."

"Well, don't miss because the next guy setting up a machine gun has a guy with him, so that's nine if none of the other men come running."

"I have my silencer, but keep me posted."

"I will. Also hurry because he's almost done setting up, and I really doubt this building will be able to withstand being shot to pieces."

Great. I had more things to worry about. "Where is the closest one?"

"You are already heading in the right direction. He should be about ten meters in front of you."

With my gun ready, I headed forward. Sure enough, there was a man standing around, waiting for his orders. They still hadn't realized that I was out there picking them off. I aimed for his skull, and a moment later, he was down.

"Next one is straight ahead, another fifteen meters."

I followed Rebecca's orders and headed forward. Another one was down without a problem. I was glad that there were birds out there still tweeting and squawking. It made it a bit easier to cover up the sound.

"Here comes the tricky part. There are two together to your one o'clock about ten meters away. You will have to be fast so they don't radio the others."

Great. I would have to aim for the second one quickly. I just prayed he wouldn't move much after I shot the first person.

I saw them in the distance and hid behind a tree. They weren't too far apart, waiting for orders. If I had a guess, the two with machine guns were to shoot up the building, and the rest would come in and finish us off. The first men must have been the few they didn't care for, checking to see if we were all in there. They should have known I was out there with that flash grenade. Apparently they weren't the brightest, but if they were working for Sebastien with no questions asked, what else would I have expected?

Aiming my gun. I shot two rounds back-to-back. Both the men went down. I let out the breath I was holding.

"Good job. Now there are three more between you

and the guy setting up. He is almost done, so if you could, like, hurry it up, that would be great."

"With three more, I don't know if I'll make it in time." Those were words that I didn't want to say. "So if you have to, use Jonathan as a shield."

"Hey!" Jonathan came on the communicator. "That is rude."

I chuckled as I moved forward. "You two have a backup plan, right?"

"Of course. But let's not get to that point. Just hurry it up."

I sighed as Rebecca led me to the next three targets. Luckily I didn't have to take more than one shot for each man. Right now I had a of bullet for every attackers left. I would hopefully have backup for the other three, but if I had to, I could potentially take them all out. I just couldn't mess up.

Which were always the last words said.

"Great. The guy with the machine gun is thirty meters straight ahead. He's al— Ah *scheiße*!"

That's when I heard it—the sound of a machine gun running. My heart felt as if it dropped as I made a run for it. With that sound, they wouldn't hear me coming.

Sure enough, there was another guy with the shooter.

I shot him in an instant, and he hit the ground next to the shooter. The shooter noticed this and began to move his gun toward me. Without hesitating, I shot him between the eyes. The machine gun stopped.

I radioed in. "Rebecca, Jonathan, are you all right? Over."

There was only static.

CHAPTER SEVENTEEN

Rebecca

I coughed as dust filled the air. We were now outside the building near the lake. I peered up to find the shooting had stopped. Jonathan had thrown a flash grenade, but I had a feeling it was Nik who had stopped him.

Taking deep breaths, I tried to get my eyes and ears focused on the surrounding forest, but everything was still a blur. My ears were ringing, and my vision was blurry. We had cut that too close.

Jonathan was up on his feet a bit faster than I was. He threw another grenade toward where I saw a couple of men going out of the tree line. I covered my ears and quickly closed my eyes. After I felt the world stop shaking, I tried to get up and hide with him behind the rubble that was now the house.

I coughed a bit, getting the dust out of my lungs. "If my calculations are correct, there should only be three more."

"Odds are that Nik will kill the one who went to see why the machine gun had stopped. So we need to capture these two alive." Jonathan pulled out his stun gun.

"Great."

"Try to get in contact with Nik. I am going to throw another grenade, and you run to the other side of them. You have your stun gun right?"

I nodded.

"Well then, I'll get the one to the left and go after the one on the right. Ready?"

I pressed the communicator. "Nik, you alive?"

"I've been trying to contact you. Why haven't you picked up?"

"Because Jonathan tried to kill us."

Jonathan shook his head.

"Did you take one out after you took out the two at the machine gun?"

"I did," Nik said.

"Then we need to take the next two alive. So don't shoot them. Well, maybe in the leg."

"Got it. Over and out."

I sighed. Jonathan motioned for me to go in three. Two. One.

I ran around the rubble that was the house. I didn't find anything on the computer, so he must have had a code ready for whenever someone visited his house. I was just glad he didn't wipe the video off the computer for the surveillance. It had come in handy.

One of the two attackers was sneaking up on the house. I slowly went around the trees and waited until I was completely behind him. He had no idea where I was. I grinned as I slowly stepped behind him, getting close enough to use my stun gun.

And when I was close enough, I fired. The electrical current hit him, causing him to start shaking and collapse to the ground. I smiled, satisfied with my mission. I grabbed the extra cuffs I had and tied him up. I also grabbed his gun.

Now Jonathan had to grab his guy, and we were all set.

I clicked my communicator. "Got mine. Any luck on your side yet?"

Moments passed as I figured Jonathan was still sneaking up to his guy. Finally he answered.

"Got him."

Nik came online. "Coming toward you, Becca."

I sighed as I sat on the ground. This was way too much excitement for my blood. But we had done it—we were in the clear.

Nik came to my aid as we lifted up the guy. We turned the channel and radioed the helicopter pilot to land near the water so we didn't have to make the entire trek back, carrying two guys. That was never easy. We also would need to inform Admiral Bardon that there was cleanup needed in these woods. Jonathan stayed behind, gathering the bodies that mainly Nik had taken down. Nik and I rode back with our two hostages. They were tied up in the back of the cargo hold.

Leaning over to me, Nik whispered in my ear, "Think they will talk?"

I shrugged. "Would it matter? They probably don't know anything."

"They could get us a name of someone we could connect to Sebastien."

"Perhaps. Or it could be another dead end. I think whatever is on the USB will be our best bet. But I wouldn't mind showing these punks who's boss and getting them to talk."

"You always did love intimidating prisoners."

"I just like seeing their scared faces. I am clearly a *Hündin* they don't want to deal with."

Nik laughed. "Ain't that a fact."

I gave him a look. "What's that supposed to mean?"

"Nothing. You just don't like people, and it shows."

"That's not true. I like some people. I like you," I said as I watched his eyes.

He turned away from me, and we didn't say anything for the rest of the trip. I shouldn't have said it, but it was true. I liked him. I even loved him. But I couldn't let him know, or it would hurt him even more in the end when he found out the truth of how I was a disgusting monster. It was going to come out sooner or later—I knew that to be a fact.

Nik and I took the prisoners to be checked in to the holding cells and went to meet with Admiral Bardon.

As he had heard of our return, he was quick to find us outside the prison area.

"I hear you two were successful." Bardon greeted us.

I nodded. "We weren't able to bring in the target, but we got his USB he had on him and brought in two of the men who were trying to kill us."

"They will be able to give us more information on how Sebastien was able to make orders from his cell. As for the USB, do you have it?"

I nodded and pulled it out of my pocket. "I'm not sure what is on it yet and am eager to find out." Mainly because it might have information of my involvement. Bardon knew that was what I'd meant.

"I'll look over it before making any official report. Meanwhile, Jonathan is doing any clean up and scanning the area. I know that Alexandra was looking for either of you earlier. Be sure to check in with her before you turn in for the day. I'll report to you in the morning what I find out on the USB."

With that, Bardon hurried off to his office, as eager as I was to find out what was stored on there. With I sigh, I turned to Nik.

"Shall we?"

He nodded, his face appearing a bit somber. I had

figured it out earlier—he didn't like visiting Walrum while I was around. I couldn't blame him, as he was my fiancée and all, or at least it had appeared that way. The fact still remained—Sebastien had implanted all the memories in him, and he didn't actually remember any of us.

And I was stuck right in the middle of this mission.

Sebastien had planned all this—and his real mission was to take down most of the head admirals for not listening to him and betraying him. If I did anything to jeopardize the mission, Nik would die. It was as simple as that. I just had to make sure everything ran smoothly on the outside.

But watching the man who called himself Walrum act as if he were the real person was beyond painful. Then watching as Nik was drowning in sorrow was even worse. Would the day come when I could tell Nik what was really going on without the risk of him being killed? I wasn't sure. All I knew was that I had to help Sebastien get out of being sentenced and help him escape after taking down all the admirals. After that, I wasn't sure what he had planned, but I had my own agenda.

And that was murdering him for everything he had

ever done to me.

We stepped inside the medical facility that Walrum was in. We checked in at the front and asked for Alexandra. Moments later, she came out from the back.

"Rebecca, Nik, I'm glad you are back in one piece."

"Thanks," I said, although I had a feeling that was directed more at Nik than me. "You wanted to see us?"

She nodded. "Follow me."

We followed her to the back of the facility where Walrum was being kept. She opened the door to the viewing room. Both Nik and I stepped inside to find Walrum eating dinner. My stomach grumbled at the sight of the food, making Nik chuckle as he handed me a granola bar. I munched on it as Alexandra began.

"As you know, Walrum is doing very well. Surprisingly well, actually. He has regained his memories from before three years ago. He has not shown any signs of aggression, relapse, and is going about his daily tasks as a normal person."

"That's great," I said, even though I knew the truth.

"Yes. It is. Which is why I am thinking tomorrow to allow him to start being able to move around the base. Not by himself, of course. And he would have to spend the night here so we can monitor him."

I frowned a little. "You want us to take care of him during the day."

She nodded her head. "Yes. I think as long as he's with you two or Jonathan during the day, he would be safe. Something outside might jog his memory and we might be able to get the information out of him. Even if we don't, it would be better for him mentally. There is no reason to keep him in here since he is no longer a threat, and I am beginning to feel a bit bad for him. He doesn't fully comprehend what happened. And although that is a good thing, I can understand how frustrating that might be to him."

I glanced over to Nik, whose face was frozen. I responded for the both of us. "That will be wonderful. I can take him for most of the day tomorrow. I have a few appointments, so Nik and Jonathan will have to take over then. But I am looking forward to it."

"Good. I am glad. Would you mind meeting here at nine?"

"I have an appointment with Bardon in the morning," I explained. "Nik, can you watch him in the morning, and I can meet up with you all at lunch?"

"Yeah. That's fine."

"Great," Alexandra said. "We will meet here

tomorrow. You two are probably tired from your mission. Go get some rest."

With that, the two of us left the room. Nik and I didn't speak a word to each other until we reached outside. It was raining again. I let out a sigh.

"That lake was so nice. Why can't we live somewhere that nice?"

He chuckled. "Because we signed up for some stupid-ass shit."

He was not in a good mood. I wanted to tell him the truth. I wanted to tell him this was all for him, but I knew that wouldn't help anyone. It would more than likely get him killed.

"I'm sorry. About everything."

Nik shook his head. "It isn't your fault. Sorry, I didn't mean what I said. I'm just glad we made it out of there fine and dandy."

"Right. Well, I am going to take a shower. Maybe see you later?"

He nodded, and I hurried off toward my room, tears stinging my eyes. As I got to my room, I opened up my drawer and stared at the vials of morphine I still had. I took long, deep breaths, wanting to break free from the mental prison I found myself in. I knew if I took it, the doctor would find out when she ran the blood tests. But I needed something—anything—to make me forget the pain I was dealing with.

Grabbing the piece of paper the doctor had given me, I dialed one of the numbers on it.

CHAPTER EIGHTEEN

Nik

This was complete and absolute shit.

I paced back and forth in my room, not sure what I was going to do next. Jonathan should be back in a couple of hours, and the moment I saw him I was going to grab him and drag him straight to a bar. Yes. That was a good plan. Because I needed something hard and I needed someone there to make sure I didn't go do something stupid.

How did this get so complicated? I sighed as I

collapsed on my bed, staring up at the ceiling. This day had been good. I felt like I had my old life back. We'd gotten a mission done, it had been exciting, and I was still shaking from all the adrenaline. I hadn't felt like that in years—even with all the trouble Rebecca and I got into. I felt as if the world would be back to normal, but I was wrong.

Because at the end of the day, Walrum was doing better and I couldn't steal the woman he had loved—the woman whom he still believed he was engaged to. I felt like a backstabbing asshole. How long did I really wait until I'd slept with Rebecca? It wasn't that long, was it? We just needed a release, and then one thing led to another, and we both ignored the demons that haunted us.

How could I have been so stupid?

I should have never listened to Jonathan—I should have never agreed to the mission. Rebecca didn't want to go on the mission, and yet I went ahead and convinced her to help take Sebastien down. If we'd just stayed as smugglers, they would have eventually been able to take him down, and Rebecca and I could have lived happily ever after.

Or Jonathan would have tried to find us again to tell

us they had found Walrum. Either way I was screwed. Rebecca and I were just not in the cards.

Unless she was going to break it off with Walrum—tell him the truth of what had happened. Did she really love him still? Who was I kidding? She loved him with all her heart. That was why we never moved forward as a couple. That was why we didn't go run and get married or make plans. Her heart died the day Walrum was killed—or had seemed to be killed. I couldn't fight for her and cause her more grief or pain.

Deciding to go check and see if Jonathan was back, I headed toward Bardon's office. Although it was sprinkling outside, it actually wasn't that bad in temperature. It was tolerable. But I had to agree with Rebecca—it had been rather nice at the lake. If we were free of this life, I would have loved to live there and watch as time passed by, not a care in the world. But that wasn't our life. No, we had missions to finish and a psychopath to take down.

I knocked on Bardon's office door. He answered from the other side. "Come in."

The door opened and I stepped inside. He appeared surprised to see me as his eyebrows rose.

"Oh, Nik. I thought you and Rebecca were with

Alexandra."

"We were," I said as I took a seat. "Apparently Walrum is well enough to start wandering around the base."

"Ah. Right. She did get permission for that."

"Do you really think it is a good idea?"

He nodded. "I do. I think it will help him regain any other memories he might have."

"Right."

Bardon leaned back. "Nik, you know there was nothing you could do, right? And that you never did anything wrong."

I frowned. "I disagree. I could have not made a move on my dead best friend's fiancé."

"There is nothing wrong with doing that though. You don't choose to love someone. Believe me, love never is a choice."

I knew that, but I couldn't convince myself that was true. "But what do I do? Do I go out and fight for her, or do I just let her run off and be happy?"

Bardon licked his lips. "I don't have an answer for that. There's no right answer. Either way, someone's heart is going to be broken and you have to choose. Will it be yours or someone else's?"

That was the problem—I didn't want anyone's heart to be broken. I rubbed my face, trying to figure out what the best answer was. I had a feeling, no matter how long I thought about it, there wouldn't be one.

"How about a distraction?" I asked. "What have you found on the USB?"

Bardon paused for a moment, as if trying to figure out what the best answer was to that. "I, uh, don't know where to start. It's information we can use, but I still need to sort through it."

He was most definitely hiding something. I didn't want to think about what that could be. I sighed. "Well, I look forward to hearing that report. Do you know when Jonathan gets back?"

Bardon checked his tablet. "He actually just landed. He will need to report to me, but I'll tell him you were looking for him."

I stood up. "Great. Tell him I'll be in my room."

"I will. And Nik, think about what I said carefully. You don't have to suffer like this."

I nodded, then left him there to meet with Jonathan.

I was lying on my bed when I heard a knock on my door.

"It's open!" I called and sat up. The door slid open to reveal Jonathan.

"You were looking for me?"

"*Ja*, want a drink?"

He examined me closely. "Does this have to do with the fact they are releasing Walrum on probation?"

"Of course," I answered with a slight smile.

He shrugged. "Sure. I'll be your designated driver of sort."

I got up and grabbed my coat. "Perfect."

We ventured to the entrance of the base and checked out. Theoretically, we could stay out the whole night, but we would have to let the men at the gate know when we left, which we didn't. Jonathan would just have to drag my sorry ass back here.

There was a bar we used to go to when we'd worked under Sebastien that we frequented. I hadn't gone back yet and was curious if the owner was still there and recognized us. The moment we stepped in, a man from behind the bar waved.

"Jonathan! Nik! How are the two of you?" Jason waved. So he did still work there.

Jonathan and I stepped up to the bar. The bar itself wasn't busy, but most of the tables were full. Jason grabbed two pint-sized glasses and filled them with our favorite dark ale. He was rough around the edges, with curly blond hair that was now graying, and a scruffy face. He was muscular but not quite as much as us since we were in the military after all. Scars covered his hands where he'd gotten into fist fights with patrons. He wasn't one who took any shit, which is why we liked him.

"Here, on the house."

"*Graci*," Jonathan said.

I nodded. *"Danke."*

He leaned forward on the bar. "So, that was crazy. I couldn't believe it when I saw the news that you two murdered the representative of Nash Mir. They sent a wanted poster for my screen, but I never posted it because I couldn't believe you four would ever do such a thing. Then when the report came out a couple of weeks ago clearing you, I was so happy."

"Well, I'm glad there were people who knew us well enough to know we were set up," I commented as I took a large swig of the ale. It was as delicious as ever. "You have no idea what kind of shit I had to drink while on the run. No beer compares to the beer here."

"You can say that again," Jonathan commented as he

downed his.

I raised an eyebrow. "And here I thought you were going to be the sober one."

"We will make it home fine. I promise. What trouble could we get into by walking a few hundred yards?"

"Knowing us, a lot."

Jason laughed. "You two haven't changed. May I ask where are the other two? I saw their names on the announcement, so I figured they were still around."

I glanced over to Jonathan. I really didn't want to talk about them. He answered for me.

"Rebecca is resting, and Walrum is still getting tests done. We will bring them around later."

"Well, I look forward to seeing them. Are the two of them still a couple?"

I should have picked somewhere that didn't have people who knew me. Jonathan was quicker to answer that one as well.

"It's complicated." He finished his drink. "Can I get another?"

"Make that two," I added as I downed my own.

Jason grabbed us two more beers, then nodded to customers at the other end of the bar. "I got to go check on my other patrons. I'll be back later."

I raised my glass in thanks and watched as he left us. I let out a long sigh.

Jonathan slapped my back. "It's all right. You haven't completely lost her yet."

"Yeah, but what do I do. To Walrum, no time has gone by since they were almost going to get married, but so much has happened since then. How do I steal someone's fiancée?"

Jonathan sipped his beer. "Have you talked to Rebecca about it all?"

"A little. But she agrees it's complicated. We need Walrum to remember what happened to him in the past three years so he can testify. I mean, we have physical evidence that he was captured and used as a science project, but we don't have evidence it was Sebastien. If we can get him to remember seeing him, then we will finally be done with it all."

"Then you can confess."

"Perhaps. I don't know, he's been through so much. How do I hurt him even more? I mean, I don't know about you, but I would be pretty devastated waking up and not remembering anything, then remembering I had a fiancée and how much I loved her and then to find out years had passed and she had found someone else."

Jonathan nodded. "True. I would be pretty mad if someone stole Jacques from me."

"Exactly. But I can't deny that I love her. I wanted to spend the rest of my life with her. I know I just need to wait it out until this trial is over, but *Gott*, it just hurts so much and I can't stop thinking about it."

Jonathan placed his hand on my back as I drank more of my beer. "Just don't worry too much about it. Focus on the mission, and after we are in the clear—after we know of everything that happened—then make your decision. A lot can happen in the next two weeks."

He was right. I downed the rest of my second beer and set my head down on the bar. "Can you order some chicken wings? I'm starving."

"Of course."

CHAPTER NINETEEN

Rebecca

Today was the big day. I sat in Bardon's office, my arms folded, as he interrogated me on how I felt. I could not wait until the person I called showed up so I didn't have to deal with this. According to the phone call yesterday, he would be in tomorrow.

The drug tests, of course, were coming along all fine and dandy. I would just need one more shot, and the doctor believed I would be in the clear. I was glad, even though I wanted more than anything to melt in the drug that was morphine. I hadn't slept well since I stopped taking it, and my nightmares were even more terrifying —but I couldn't tell anyone that. If they knew what I saw in my night terrors, they would get me a real psychologist, and I wanted the one I had called last night.

"So, are you ready for today?" Bardon asked.

I shrugged. "I guess? I mean, it's still strange he's alive. But I think it will be good for him mentally to get out of that cell."

Bardon nodded. "Right. That's it?"

"What do you want from me? You know a good chunk of my past. I don't exactly show my emotions."

"I know. And that's not good."

"No, it's called having to finish missions no matter the cost." I gave him a smile. "Speaking of which, what did you find on that USB?"

Bardon scratched his forehead. "A lot of stuff. Stuff I couldn't believe. Lots of stuff with you."

"Meaning it's going to be hard to pull any evidence against me out of it."

"Yup. Sebastien is using you as leverage it seems. It was why he kept him alive—all the evidence he had pulled you down with him."

"And he must have figured out you had a soft spot for me. Interesting. I wonder how he was led to believe that. Must have been all the times you came up to us and talked to me."

Bardon pinched the bridge of his nose. "Look, I know this is my fault in that sense. I was just worried. I didn't know he could be that devious."

I shook my head. "Welcome to my life. Do you think there is anything on there that we can point just toward him?"

"Yeah. It's just going to take me some time. Most of it are photos, all of which you are in. Any of our IT officers will be able to spot if I mess with those."

"Right. That would explain why he always wanted me so close on missions. I figured it was because he was so possessive."

"I have a feeling it was probably a bit of both."

We sat there for a few moments. I checked the clock. It was almost noon now. "I am supposed to go meet Nik and Jonathan to take over watching Walrum."

"Are you sure you are prepared for this?"

"I have been meeting with him every day, so this shouldn't be any different."

Bardon waved at me. "Fine. If you have any

problems, just come find me. I'll be in the interrogation area with Jonathan and Nik this afternoon as we are going to talk to the two men you captured yesterday."

"Sounds good. If you need any help with that, let me know."

"I'd rather you not interrogate them, just in case they recognize you."

I nodded. "That's a fair point. Well then, I'll see you later. *Bis bald.*"

"*À plus.*"

I left Bardon's office and headed straight toward the cafeteria where I would meet up with Nik and Walrum. I took a deep breath as I stepped outside. It was muggy today—another hot day with a lot of moisture in the air. I couldn't wait to move out of here to somewhere nicer, even though Regenswelt was my home and the place I loved so much. It was strange thinking this place was home when I had been on the move most of my life. Perhaps I was getting soft.

Passing by the prison area, I felt my stomach wrench. I knew Sebastien was in there, waiting for his trial. I hadn't gone to any of the interrogations as I didn't want to see his face. I didn't want to remember all the things he had made me do and all things I would be doing to make sure he escaped this place. I let out a sigh, knowing what I was going to do was wrong, but it was the only way to make sure Nik stayed safe. Then I would take my revenge out on him myself.

I entered the cafeteria, and for a moment it felt like old times. Walrum, Nik, and Jonathan were all seated at the table we used to claim as our own. I took a long, deep breath and tried to stay sane. Nothing about this was normal. Nothing about this was healthy. It was all one toxic web of lies.

"Hey. How did it go?" I asked in a slightly cheerful voice.

Jonathan nodded. "Good. We showed him around. He seems to remember most of the necessary areas."

"I know my own home." Walrum grinned. "At least the place I had spent most of my life. We never really have a home, do we?"

Fucked-up minds think alike. "Someday, perhaps. Let me grab something to eat, and then I'll relieve the two of you."

"Yeah, go get your rabbit food," Jonathan called after me. I shook my head, smiling a little but not letting him see that. I did miss that, but I knew it wasn't real.

I grabbed a salad and some tofu, which really was

rabbit food, and took a seat. I nodded to Nik.

"Hey, how are the sessions going with your eye?"

His eye widened. "Oh, it was going to be a surprise, but I only need one more session and I can take the eye patch off. It's getting a lot better but still healing. Tomorrow, actually, I should be good to go."

"That's great! We will have to celebrate. Shall we go out for drinks? Is our bar still open?"

Jonathan and Nik glanced at each other. "Yeah," Jonathan answered. "We checked on it last night. We should go there tomorrow."

"Great! Then it's a plan."

Nik nodded as he stood up with his tray. "We better get going. I know Bardon had some things he needed us for."

"Have fun!" I called after them. I glanced over to Walrum, who was still smiling. Even though I knew it wasn't really him inside, I couldn't help but blush a little. He used to smile like that when we were alone. But this thing didn't know that.

"They are some really strange bastards, aren't they?"

I glanced around, making sure no one heard. "Shh. Someone might hear you. We can go to my room to talk later. No one would find that suspicious since we did used to be engaged."

He grabbed my hand. "Still are, technically."

I wanted to retract my hand and slap him. There was no way I would marry this empty shell of a man—not unless his memories actually were restored. Right now he was just a puppet for Sebastien—a puppet I helped maneuver into getting the others to trust him. I sighed.

"Right. For the mission's sake."

He held up a finger. "Ah, ah, ah. No talk of that until we are somewhere else."

"Right. Sorry. Let me finish up eating, and we can have our little meeting," I mumbled as I stuffed some lettuce in my mouth.

"But I have to ask, you and Nik were a thing, weren't you? He seems pretty mad and frustrated when he's around me."

I glared at the man. "That is none of your concern."

He laughed but stayed silent for the rest of the time I ate. Even though my stomach hurt from the worry and resentment that all this was causing me, I still managed to finish my lunch. Grabbing my tray, I put my dirty dishes away and led Walrum to my room. No one seemed to be back in their quarters, as it was midday, so I knew no one was going to hear the conversation we were about to have.

The door slid shut behind Walrum, and I sighed.

"So, what's next in this horrible, horrible plan, hmm? I presume Sebastien programed you or whatever for each step."

He bit. "I can see why my former self liked you so much. You're fiery."

I crossed my arms. "I could kill you and save me the trouble of dealing with this mission."

He shrugged. "Then your darling Nik dies. Do you really want to be all alone in this world?"

I let out a huff. "*Was immer*. Just tell me what is next."

Walrum took a seat on my small couch. I was still amazed that Nik was able to sleep on that thing as it was quite small.

"Well, we keep up the act of being engaged. I make it seem like I'm almost at full recovery and beginning to remember the past three years. Then it will seem that I can be a witness for the trial. The trial will then proceed, and we take out each and every one there."

"Except for Nik," I commented.

"Except for your beloved Nik, who will watch you murder a bunch of government officials and have no real life after this. *Ja*, I know."

I frowned. He had a good point there. But little did they know I was working on a plan of my own. "When will you start confessing about what happened?"

He placed his finger on his chin. "I was thinking early next week. It would be perfect timing."

So four more days. I could live with that. The psychologist I called would be here tomorrow evening and all would be swell. According to him, he was going to be talking to Sebastien and Walrum as well, and he really was one of the best.

I knew Sebastien would not be happy that Admiral Rolf Jørgensen was the one called in, as he and Rolf has some kind of feud going on. I could lie and say I didn't know why that was, but who was I kidding? It was because Rolf had no problem undermining Sebastien and taking anything out from under him.

Walrum leaned back. "Now, how about you fill me in with everything I need to know about my past life that was hidden from Sebastien?"

CHAPTER TWENTY

Nik

It had been a while since I sat in on an interrogation—or at least one that actually went somewhere. I had sat in when they first started questioning Sebastien, but they didn't get anything out of him. I stopped going to those because he stayed silent and it didn't go anywhere. And it frustrated me to no end.

But today we had two men who would break at lot easier than Sebastien. If it came down to it, I could go in there and help question, but I would just watch from the sidelines behind the one-way mirror with Jonathan and Bardon until I was needed. Bardon had sent Burt in to question him. Apparently, Burt was good at getting people to talk. I couldn't wait to see this.

"So, in looking at your file, it says you are a mercenary. Did you work for anyone?"

The man nodded. "That's right. I was given a job, and I went to execute it."

"Did you realize how dangerous it was before you went in?" Burt asked. So far it was rudimentary questions to throw him off guard.

"Every mission is a risk. Did I think that three people could take out our sixteen? No."

"So you knew there were three who you needed to execute?"

The man paused. "We were told there were four, and the house and electronics needed to be destroyed."

"Great," I commented. "They knew it was us who were there. It sure wasn't them keeping watch on the area. They knew specifics of the mission."

Jonathan let out a sigh. "That means this was a setup. But who could have leaked the information?"

Bardon crossed his arms but didn't say a word. I had a feeling he wanted to say it was Rebecca, but that didn't make sense as she was almost killed as well. She wouldn't want any of us dead. No, this was someone else. Sebastien had his tentacles everywhere.

"I think the pilot could have been in on it. Or perhaps he mentioned to someone he was taking us, not thinking about it."

Bardon shook his head. "It doesn't matter who it is—what's nerve-racking is that they moved in that quickly. I figured since I made and gave you the mission so fast we wouldn't have to worry. I also figured it would have been them keeping visuals on the place, not that they were specifically after you three."

He had a good point. The fact that Sebastien was able to put together this mission against us so quickly from behind bars was not a good sign. He had men everywhere.

Burt went on interrogating. "So you and your men were hired to execute four people. Were you given names? Photos?"

"We were given photos an hour before the mission was to be executed."

"Did you have any idea that they were all part of the military?"

He laughed. "If I did, I would have thought twice

before taking the job."

"Why did you take the job? Was the contact someone you already knew?"

The man leaned back in his hair, his wrists bound to the table in front of him. "I do not disclose that information to anyone."

Bardon tapped his hand on his tablet. "We are lucky—this man doesn't realize he revealed he was their leader. And we are lucky that you guys captured the leader."

"The leader is always the last one to go in the front. The odds weren't too much against us," Jonathan commented.

I nodded in agreement as Burt continued.

"You do realize you tried to kill military officers. If you give us the name of your employer, you'll get a lighter sentence—maybe even released without incident. Our admiral here is pretty generous if people will talk." Burt leaned on the table across from him. "But only if one cooperates."

The man shrugged. "I don't know what you want from me. Part of the deal is secrecy. Even if I reveal who it is, my life is ruined and no one will hire me."

"But at least you wouldn't be in a jail cell. You could

always find a different job." Burt started pacing and scratching his chin. "I don't know about your friend though. Seems to me he doesn't have any information worth giving since you made it clear you don't reveal any of the contact information to your employees. That's too bad; he seems pretty young."

The man didn't say anything, but it was clear on his face that he didn't like the sound of that as his eyes narrowed. "He's a good kid."

Burt shrugged. "But he tried to kill some military officers. And that's highly frowned upon in these parts. Even if you got out, you probably wouldn't have anyone work with you since you couldn't save any of your men, and the one who didn't get killed will be in prison for the rest of his life, all because he followed orders. I don't know about you, but that's got to hurt your reputation for getting men to work for you."

"Doesn't matter," the man said. "Because I won't talk and will be in jail the rest of my life as well."

Burt laughed. "Is that so? Do you fear your employer more than you do a jail cell? Because let me tell you, the officers who watch our prisoners aren't very kind to those who tried to kill our men, if you catch my drift. Especially if they are young."

"He seems to have a soft spot for the other prisoner we have. Luck is definitely on our side this time," Bardon said with a slight sigh.

Jonathan nodded. "Yeah. It explains why he was with him and moved in last. I just wonder if it will be enough and whether we can trace his employer back to Sebastien in any way."

"Probably not," I mumbled. "I'm not sure if you noticed, but he makes sure to cut any loose ends. The guy he names is probably dead in a ditch somewhere."

"That's more than likely true. But we can look him up in our records and start connecting dots," Bardon explained.

I chuckled. "If you try to connect a bunch of dots together, it will be like those rooms with all the red string. But then it would be a bunch of knots and just really crazy."

Jonathan nodded. "That's for sure. One would go crazy with all the loose ends. I know that I am."

The man finally spoke. "I can't tell you who he is. That's the end of the story."

Burt shrugged. "All right. Don't come crying to me when you find out the truth about what is going on. And when the wards start beating you up and you realized you made a grave mistake, there will be no turning back."

"But if I reveal the information to you, will you be able to guarantee my safety? Because I can promise you that they will send people after me and I'll die the moment I set foot out of here."

"That all depends on who your employer was. If he has any connection with the man we are trying to take down, then he will be executed and you won't have to worry. But then again, I don't know who contacted you."

The man let out a slow breath. "I can't. I don't want to die."

"Fine then. Guards, take him away and bring me the other one."

"Wait, he doesn't know anything?"

Burt shrugged again. "I can't know that for certain, can I? No, I have to figure that out myself. That is, unless you have a name?"

He gritted his teeth. I was curious if he was going to spill. Most mercenaries took a bit longer to crack. The man turned away. I guess I was right—Burt would just have to deal with the other one first and give the commander a little more desperation.

Jonathan turned to me. "So, seems that is going to take a little more time. But Nik, you said your eye patch is going to come off tomorrow?"

I nodded. "Yup. I'll have my eye back tomorrow. Crazy, I never thought I was ever going to be able to use it again."

"That will be great. We will definitely have to celebrate."

I sort of smiled, sort of frowned. Jonathan rolled his eyes. "You will have to get used to being around Walrum and Rebecca sooner or later. Besides, would you even want to celebrate without Rebecca?"

I shook my head. "No, I wouldn't. I just need some time to see how all this plays out. I'll try to act fine tomorrow."

Bardon glanced between the two of us but didn't say anything. He knew this was complicated and more than likely didn't want to touch it.

"Well, it seems to me that Burt has this handled," I said, wanting to change the subject. "What do you need us for?"

"I want you to see if you can spot any hint of Sebastien being involved. So far, due to how scared the commander is, I would guess it does have something to do with him. I'm just having a problem figuring out how he is involved."

Bardon had a point. More eyes on what was going on in that room the better. Burt didn't know the whole story, or at least I didn't think he did. He didn't know of all the crimes that were pinned on Sebastien or how we were undercover for the majority of our lives. He didn't know the things that bastard set us up for. All he knew was that he needed to find the truth and take a bad man down.

The younger assailant was brought in. His eyes were red as if he had been crying. I didn't know if that was because he had lost friends in their mission or if it was because he was afraid for his life. Perhaps it was both.

He sat down and stared at the table before him. Yeah, he was most definitely crying in fear for his life and from the shock of everything that happened. Burt slammed his hands down on the table before him. The man jumped and almost fell out of his chair.

"Do you have any idea how much trouble you are in?"

The man quickly shook his head. "N-no sir."

"You tried to kill an officer in the military. You and your comrades took out an important witness to a trial.

Do you have any idea how long your sentences will be? I'll give you a clue." Burt leaned in. "You won't be seeing the sky ever again."

The man started crying. "I didn't know our targets were military. We wouldn't have taken the job. The boss said it was a simple mission, just to take out some criminals. We were lied to."

I raised an eyebrow. "Criminals? That was interesting. The fact was, we were originally, so either the employer lied or was using past information. I had a feeling it was the former.

"Who was your employer?" Burt asked.

The man shook his head. "I have no idea. I'm not given that information. Please! I didn't know! I was just doing as I was told."

I knew that feeling. That was how the four of us were set up for the murder we were arrested for. We were sent to the wrong place at the wrong time. Or more like we were sent there so we would get in trouble.

"He doesn't know anything. Bring in the other guy. If he sees his friend crying like this, he might confess," I said.

"I'm going to give it a day. Burt will threaten him some more. If he has the night to sit on it all, he will be able to convince the other to talk. But you are right. He doesn't know anything. You don't need to be here any longer. Feel free to take the rest of the day off."

I nodded. I really didn't have anything else to do, but I decided to go train on my own. It had been a while since I had a full workout anyway.

CHAPTER TWENTY-ONE

Rebecca

Tonight could not come soon enough. I sat in the doctor's office, waiting for my results to come in. Odds were that I was pretty clean even though it took everything in me not to grab a vial and sleep into bliss. The only reason I hadn't was because they would find out right away and Bardon would scold me—I really hated being scolded—and because my drug that I wanted would be arriving tonight.

It was selfish of me to call on Rolf even though he

was already heading out this way. It was more selfish because if the others knew his and my relationship, they would judge me. Granted, he and I never had a tryst when I was dating Walrum nor when I was dating Sebastien. But there had been some in-between time where he and I hooked up a few times. A week.

And now I wanted more than anything to just let go and have a nice night.

It wasn't as if I could have sex with Walrum since he was still the brainwashed creature that Sebastien had made him into. Then I couldn't have sex with Nik, or he would crack, thinking he'd betrayed Walrum, so that left Rolf.

And he was a therapist, so perhaps we could talk a little and make Bardon happy. Rolf knew things about me that none of the others did, as he and I had talked a bit about my past before. He was good at getting information out of me. I didn't like that about him.

The doctor stepped back in the room. Her face was lit up. "You are clear! Have you noticed any symptoms?"

I shook my head. "Nein, I haven't. I have been feeling pretty good actually. Admiral Bardon and I have been talking, and I think that has helped a lot."

Truthfully, it probably did. Knowing someone was

there, wanting to help me, thinking I was innocent, helped a little. Then the guilt set in and I was back to my old self. I also couldn't tell her that my night terrors had been about the same. I didn't think any amount of anything would make those go away.

"That is great. I heard Admiral Dr. Jørgensen is in town today. I'm sure he would love to help you with anything you have been struggling with."

I smiled a little. "I'm sure he would. I'll talk to him when he arrives."

"That's great to hear. I was worried you wouldn't talk to anyone, but it seems Admiral Bardon has softened you up a bit."

"Something like that."

"Well, if you need anything else, don't hesitate to come in here. I don't think you need to check in anymore unless something is wrong. But I want to note that if you ever take morphine-B again, there is a high chance that the serum won't work. Due to the amount you took, your body was affected by it a lot. I have put in your charts that doctors will need to use something else if the time came. Just stay out of dangerous situations."

I had a feeling that was going to bite me in the ass in

the future. But I would deal with that later. "So I'm free?"

"You are free." She laughed.

Which meant I could potentially start taking the morphine again. I knew that shouldn't have been my first thought, but knowing that, if need be, I could get away with it was a relief. That is, until I needed to get off it. But perhaps I could sneak some of the serum out myself or have someone else do it. Either way, I should be somewhat clear. If the time came.

I got up and started for the door when a thought hit me. "Oh, when is Nik going to be in for his eye appointment? Today is his last one, right?"

She nodded. "That it is. His appointment is just after lunch. He should be done around three if you want to come for the big reveal."

"Thanks. I might just do that." I turned and left.

It was great that Nik had been getting his eye fixed, but I had wished he would have told me when the appointments were. Then again, I didn't tell him about my own appointments, so I presumed we were even. If I were honest, I would probably have skipped out as I didn't like coming to the doctors. I was starting to get used to it now, but earlier I stayed away from this place.

Now I had to go pick up Walrum. I wasn't looking forward to that. He was himself when he was around me, meaning he wasn't the sweet Walrum I once had known. No, he was the shell of the man I'd known, filled with hatred and orders. There was no humanity in him, just whatever Sebastien had installed.

And it was the worst thing imaginable.

Yesterday made me want to snap and use my morphine, maybe even enough to go to sleep for good, but I knew better. I knew if I killed myself, Nik would pay the price and be killed. I wouldn't be able to see his lovable grin or hear his delightful smile. No, I would be gone and he would be soon after. Then who knew what would have happened next for Sebastien. Knowing my luck, he would probably get away.

Today Walrum was still in the lab facility, waiting to be released from his room or cell, depending on how you looked at it. I checked in at the front as I always did, but before they released him, Alexandra wanted to talk to me. I didn't like the sound of that, but I kept my face blank, as I normally did, and headed to where she would be studying brain scans and the like. The attendant escorted me to the room, and when the door slid open, I found one stressed-out scientist staring at screens.

"Whoa," I commented as I saw the dark rings around her eyes and her fingers gripping her scalp. Her hair was a mess, and I peered back, wondering if I could make a run for it.

She glanced at me. "Oh, Rebecca, what are you doing here so late?"

I peered up at the clock. "Um, it's nine in the morning."

Her head whipped to the clock. "*Blyad*! I did it again." She sighed as she grabbed her coffee and sipped. "Sorry, I guess the night got away from me."

"Apparently. What have you been doing?" I asked as I made my way closer to her.

She slid her finger on the screen. "I've been looking at the brain scans from when Walrum first came in here versus yesterday."

"Oh?" Not that I knew anything about brain scans.

"There's nothing different about them. I mean, the activity is a bit different, indicating less anger, but that is it. But he has made a complete one-eighty. It makes no sense."

Because he was still the asshole we brought in. "I know nothing about any of this. I just see weird images of brains on your screen.”

She let out a sigh. “I know, I know. I just can't figure out the solution to all of this. I don’t know how to get evidence from Walrum to show the court. What I thought was brain damage clearly isn’t, and something else is going on.”

“I couldn’t tell you.”

She stood up. “I guess he is good to go out for the day.”

“We are going to a bar this evening with Nik and Jonathan. Is it fine to bring him with?”

She nodded. “Yeah, just check him out at the front and keep an eye on him. But there is no reason that I can see to not allow him to go with you. He has his memories and is doing good.”

The memories Sebastien and I gave him. “Great. I’ll have him back after dinner then.”

“I guess I’ll see what Admiral Dr. Jørgensen says. He is going to interview him in the next couple of days.”

“That’s what I heard.”

“Do you know the admiral?”

“Oh yeah, we go way back. He has been a great help.”

“Well, that is good to hear. I haven’t met the man, but

I have heard good things. He is said to be one of the best."

I agreed he was one of the best that I knew. He was good at what he did, no matter what that was. I tried not to think about the times we had spent together, as I knew my cheeks would turn red.

"Have any plans for the day then? With Walrum, I mean."

I shook my head. "Nope. Maybe some training, walk around the compound. Not much to do when you don't have a mission and aren't technically a captain anymore."

"Right. Well, have fun."

"Danke schon."

Walrum was released to my care, and I greeted him with a kiss on the cheek, trying to appear like a fiancée would. It had been so long I wasn't sure I could really act the way I had back then with this skinwalker. We stepped outside, and I let out a sigh.

"Is it really that horrible to be around me? And here I thought you loved me."

"I loved Walrum. I don't know who you are. I don't even think you have a soul in there."

He shrugged. "I don't think I do either. Not that I

understand what a soul really is."

I couldn't argue with that. No one really knew what a soul was. It was almost like ancient myth. Some people believed in the afterlife, but I believed only things that I could fight. If there was a god, I wouldn't care because he or she hadn't been there to save me from the demon that was Sebastien.

Turning to Walrum, I tried to appear as if I cared. "So, *meine Leibe*, what do you want to do today?"

He shrugged. "Whatever you want to do, *mein Schatz*."

I let out a breath. "I guess some physical training, lunch, stay in my room going over more random *scheiße*, and then meet up with Nik for his eye surgery?"

"Sounds fine to me. But should you really take your fiancée along to see the man you have been fucking?"

I dug my nails into my palm. "I mean, I could just tell him what you really are. Fuck up your entire plan."

"Then he will die."

I turned away from him. "Yeah, yeah. Whatever. Let's go."

CHAPTER TWENTY-TWO

Nik

The first thing I saw when they unwrapped my eye was Rebecca. The second thing I saw was Walrum wrap his arm around her waist.

I didn't expect her to come to the doctor's office after my surgery. We were planning to meet up after and go have dinner and drinks. Never could I have imagined that she would be waiting for me like this. And if it weren't for the fact Walrum was also there, it would have been perfect.

She smiled at me. "Oh, Nik, I am so happy for you! You have no idea!"

I did know. She, for some reason, felt responsible for the damage that was caused by my eye. I moved my hand to touch the skin around it. There were bumps from the scars that were still there, but at least I could see.

It was strange. I had figured out how to adjust for the lost sight for so long that everything around me seemed so much clearer now. I glanced around, wondering how I could have forgotten such a big difference. I guess I learned to adapt.

"Your eyes were always so beautiful," Rebecca commented. "I am glad you were finally able to get it healed."

I blushed a little and glanced away. Now was not the time to appear in love—not when her fiancée was standing right there.

"Where's Jonathan?"

Rebecca shrugged. "*Ich weiß nicht.* I ain't his keeper. He's probably working with Bardon on something. Wasn't Burt going to interrogate those mercenaries again today?"

Right. I had forgotten about that. "Yeah, we should

probably go meet up with him, and then we can go grab dinner after."

She nodded. "*Ja,* I would like to see Burt interrogate someone. I mean, I would spill all my secrets if I had to be in a room with him. He annoys the heck out of me."

I got off the table chair thing and turned to the doctor. "Am I good to go?"

Dr. Theissi nodded. "Yup. Just take it easy. You do need to check out in the front, however."

I nodded and did just that. As I left with Rebecca and Walrum, I leaned over to her.

"Didn't I hear that you challenged Burt to a fight and won?"

She grinned. "That I did."

"But then you lost to Jonathan."

She let out a sigh and rolled her eyes. "That was a one-time thing. He got the better of me because I had been training and fighting for over an hour. He simply waltzed in and acted like he owned the place. Pissed me off to no end."

"Oh, I bet. He was talking about it for days—how he beat the amazing Rebecca. Honestly, I didn't believe it. But then I remembered he'd gotten to stay here and train while he was in hiding, and you and I only had gotten to train on a tight ship."

"I don't recall you complaining," she mumbled under her breath.

I couldn't believe she said that. I glanced over to Walrum, who didn't seem to notice her comment. Thank *Gott* for that.

"So, did they find anything out yesterday from those two guys we brought in?"

I shook my head. "No names, but we do know one of them is the leader and has a soft spot for the other guy. We are hoping to use that against them. That was their hope for today."

"Well, that sounds perfect. If we get the name, we can see who it links back to."

I nodded. "Yeah, hopefully. But knowing Sebastien, it will probably be a wild-goose chase."

"You can say that again."

We made it to the interrogation area and found Bardon and Jonathan discussing something outside the front. When we arrived, they quickly ended their conversation.

"How did it go?" I asked.

Jonathan glanced at Bardon. "Good. But we can't discuss any further with Walrum. He still isn't clear for mission reports."

Scheiße, that was right. Hopefully I hadn't said anything with him around that I wasn't supposed to. "Well, we were thinking of getting dinner. Admiral Bardon, would you like to join us?"

He shook his head. "No, I still have some business to finish up. Go have fun, but be sure to bring my man back at a reasonable time." He wrapped his arm around Jonathan's waist and kissed him on the cheek.

"Well, I can't promise anything." I smiled. "You know how Jonathan can get."

Jonathan made his most innocent "*who, me?*" look he could muster. I rolled my eyes as we turned to head to the entrance of the base.

"By the way, Nik, you look dashing with both your eyes. The giant scar just adds to your rough look you have going. Everyone will be afraid of you on missions."

That's all I ever wanted—more people afraid of me. "Maybe I want to look normal and fit in."

"That ship sailed long ago when you joined the military." Jonathan elbowed me in the side. "Besides, don't the ladies like a man who has a story?"

I glanced at Rebecca, who seemed to be looking

away. I had hoped she would overhear and show some kind of jealousy. I supposed I was mistaken.

We made it to the entrance and checked out. They had to double-check with Alexandra to make sure Walrum was free to leave the base under supervision. She gave her okay, and we were off toward our regular hangout.

"Freedom at last." Rebecca stretched her arms out. "I hate being stuck on the base all day."

"You do realize you can leave, right? As long as you check out and stay in town."

"Yeah, true, but it's a lot less fun when you are alone. Besides, I don't like to come out here on my own. Just because it was broadcasted that we were innocent for the ordeal with the Nash Mir representative, that doesn't mean people aren't still going to take it out on us. And there's the whole Sebastien wanting all of us dead thing."

"Right," I commented. "That."

Jonathan shrugged. "And we already proved that we can take them out if need be. Not even an army of mercenaries can take us out."

I laughed. "That's a fact. Although we didn't have to worry about civilians around us. It could have gone a lot worse if we were trying to save others. We didn't even save our target."

Jonathan turned to Rebecca. "And whose fault is that?"

"Bastard almost broke my nose. It was his fault for running. But if he hadn't, I might have been killed too." She held her hand up. *"C'est la vie."*

"You are one cold *chienne*, you know that, right?"

She nodded and gave us her most innocent smile. *"Jawohl."*

"I see things haven't changed," Walrum interjected. "You two never did get along."

Jonathan slapped Rebecca's back. "I like to call it being playful with friends. What do you say, Rebecca?"

She moved his arm. "I call it someone who gets on my nerves. But I have to admit, I'd rather have you around than those kids you hired for the mission. But then again, you knew I didn't like working with other people, and you still hired them. Some friend you are."

"Je suis désolé, you know how things go. We had to get across the border somehow. Besides, they were very helpful in the end."

"Whatever happened to them all? I mean, they all seemed that they were involved in the military in one shape or form," I asked.

"Well," Jonathan began. "Alexandra and Burt are on the base, as you know. Mary, Russ, and Samuel are working on another base as they requested working on some ships or whatnot."

"Are Mary and Samuel still dating?" Rebecca asked.

He shrugged. "No idea. I don't talk to them. Why do you care?"

She shook her head. "I don't, just curious. Young love and all that is oh so sweet and innocent."

"Not that you would know, right?" Jonathan jested.

"Nope. Nothing innocent about any of my loves."

I gave Jonathan a look. He simply grinned at me as we entered the bar.

The bar wasn't too packed—just about normal for that time of day. Most of the men on the base who could leave were here, along with some civilians. Jason was working behind the bar again and waved at us.

"You are all here!" He came out from behind the bar. "And just your luck—your old table is open."

"Perfect," I commented as he led us to the back of the bar.

"Walrum, I am so glad to see you. I was worried something might have happened," Jason said as we made it to the table.

I watched Walrum's face. He appeared confused—as if he wasn't sure how to respond. I thought perhaps it was because he didn't know how to say I was locked up in some asshole's laboratory for three years, but it was more like he didn't know what to say because he didn't know who this man was.

"Uh, yeah. I'm fine. *Danke*."

Jason peered as perplexed as I did. Jonathan narrowed his eyes but said nothing.

"It's me! Jason. Do you not recognize me?"

Walrum laughed and gestured to his head. "I lost part of my memory, sorry. There are things here and there I remember, but I guess it's not fully back yet. Sorry."

Jason's eyes widened. "I am so sorry to hear that. I presume you are getting better though?"

Walrum nodded. "Yes, I am. Hopefully soon those will come back to me." His eyes flickered to Rebecca who said nothing, but I could tell her jaw was tight.

What in the world was going on there?

CHAPTER TWENTY-THREE

Rebecca

I'd forgotten about Jason working there. So much time had passed. I figured he was gone, and it just simply slipped my mind.

But I had a feeling Walrum, or whatever he was, was going to blame me for not releasing that information to him. I was not looking forward to that. It didn't matter, because he was supposed to have amnesia. Most people with amnesia forgot random things.

Except some of the memories he had referenced so far were in this bar. Oops.

I glanced at Nik and Jonathan. They were studying Walrum. I had a feeling, due to what Alexandra had told me about the brain scans, they were suspicious about him. I would just have to play along with it all. Or else Nik's life could be my punishment.

"Even after all this time, Jason, I bet you still remember our favorite drinks." I changed the topic.

He nodded with a wide grin. "That I do! Four dark ales, your favorite brand?"

Walrum held up his hand. "Just three. I am not allowed to drink quite yet."

Jason made a thumbs-up and went behind the bar to grab our drinks. Everyone was quiet. I guessed it had been some time since we were all together like this.

"So," I began. "It seems Jason is doing well."

Nik nodded. "Yeah, we came here the other day, and he recognized us right away. It's nice to know there were some people in our past life who believed we were innocent."

I cocked an eyebrow. "He didn't believe the wanted signs for treason or whatever?"

"Nope," Jonathan answered. "This whole time we could have hidden at this bar."

I laughed. "Right, not like there's a bunch of military officers here who would recognize us or anything."

Nik rolled his eyes. "Could you imagine? We would probably only survive here for like, a minute."

"A minute?" I asked. "Speak for yourself. I could probably take everyone here. I would last at least fifteen minutes. Until they brought in a machine gun. Even then I might last a bit longer."

"Sure," Jonathan commented.

"I would."

"And yet you were captured at the border," Walrum commented. We all glanced at him. "Or at least that is what you said to me."

I actually did tell him about the mission to take down Sebastien. "Yeah, yeah, but I let them capture me. In fact, they were going to beat me up, and I escaped them all so…" I shrugged. "My case still stands."

Jason brought the round of drinks and water for Walrum and set them on the table. "Would you all like to order food?"

Luckily, Jason made sure there was some food on the menu that I could eat—sourdough sandwich with all vegan ingredients. I, since it was the only thing I could eat, ordered that. The others looked through the menu as they had options to choose from.

"I'll take the chicken wings again. With some fries," Nik ordered.

Jonathan scratched his chin. "I'll take the beer-and-cheese soup."

"And I'll take the french-dip sandwich. With fries as well."

I held up my hand. "I also want fries. As long as they aren't fried in the same oil as meat."

"They are not. Coming right up. Let me know if you need anything else. We start getting busy right about now, so I'll be moving around a lot."

With that, he hurried off. He really needed to hire more helpers, as he only had two waiters and about twenty tables. Then again, I had never run a business before. It seemed to be working for him though, so I supposed it was fine.

"So, Nik." I turned my attention back to my comrades. "What's it like being able to see out of both eyes after all this time?"

He fiddled with his hands on the table. "Strange. It's like I never realized what I was missing or how different visually everything had been. But it's nice. It feels as if things are going back to normal after all this time, if that is even possible."

I was being controlled by a madman—so I definitely felt like things were back to normal. I took a gulp of my beer. My eyes widened. "Oh man, it has been way too long since I had beer, let alone beer this good."

"Oh, that's right," Jonathan commented as he sipped his own drink. "You couldn't have alcohol while being on that drug."

We all went silent for a moment. I nodded a little. "Yeah, I couldn't."

Nik seemed to be lost in thought. He was more than likely thinking of all the times we had been drinking. He didn't say anything though, for which I was glad. I hated that I had lied to him for so long, and I wanted to forget about it.

And I was still lying to him—I had made him think it was all okay when it wasn't. No, this was far from over.

"So," Walrum began, trying to fit in, or at least that was what it appeared to me. "We used to hang out here a lot. I remember it a bit, but that man. Jason was it? Was he always around?"

Jonathan nodded. "Yeah. He's a friend of sorts. He

dotes on us, which is why we always spent time here."

I laughed. That was true. "We used to play darts over there quite a bit. And pool in the game room."

Walrum began to stand up. "Well then, let's do that while we wait for our food? Let's see who is still the best at those games."

I hadn't told him we played those games, so he actually didn't know who usually won. He was playing it up as if he did know, however. It was a smart move.

And, naturally, I was usually the winner at both those games.

"Let's make it interesting and bet on it." I grinned. "Let's say, twenty credits each?"

Jonathan laughed. "If you want. I have to be honest, I didn't have much to do while we were in hiding, Rebecca. I spent most of that time playing pool."

I raised an eyebrow as we made our way across the bar. "Oh? So you might actually stand a chance against me? I'll have to be honest, there were a few business transactions that only had a good outcome because I beat them at pool."

Nik nodded. "It's true. We probably would have been shot if it weren't for her skills. Although other times her winning was the reason we got beat up and tossed out of bars."

I laughed. "Good times, good times."

I went to the table and clicked a few buttons. The balls materialized on the table. I grabbed a cue and gave it a good looking over, making sure none of the electronic sensors were damaged. I didn't need to be screwed over, especially not in this game.

"Who wants to break?" I asked.

Jonathan gestured to the table. *"Les dames d'abord."*

I lined up my cue. "I am anything but a lady, but I'll take it."

After breaking, we went around, trying to hit each number in a row. If you hit the wrong number in, it was a negative point. By the time food came around, I was winning seven to six to four to four. Theoretically Jonathan could hit the last one in and tie, but with how I set up my last shot, it was an impossible task.

Jason set the food on our table, and we waved at him that we would be right there. I turned back to the game.

"Come on, Jonathan, weren't you going to teach me how good you got?"

"Tais-toi, I am working on it."

He took the shot, but it bounced off the edge of the corner and didn't go in.

"Aww, so sad." I turned to Nik. "Nik, your turn!"

"Thanks for setting me up, *guter Freund*." Nik began lining up the shot.

"I see you lot are still as loud as ever," a voice said behind me, causing Nik to fumble and miss his shot. Jonathan laughed at him as I turned around to find Rolf standing behind me.

"Admiral Dr. Jørgensen. It has been a long time," I said.

He nodded, his graying brown hair loosely styled back, as some of his bangs still masked his forehead. Rolf glanced at the pool table. "Oh, I'm sorry, did I make you miss your shot, Nik?"

Nik shrugged. "I was going to lose either way, so no worries."

I grinned. "I'm going to win a bunch of money tonight. I'm pretty excited."

Walrum didn't say anything as he made the shot. It went in, giving him five points.

"Well, there we go. Looks like I won, Jonathan. You owe me."

Jonathan stuck his tongue out at me. I chuckled as I put my cue away.

"It seems you all are getting back to normal," Rolf

commented. "I hope I'll see you around the base. I just got in and was grabbing a bite to eat."

Nik nodded. "Definitely. I'm sure we will see you later this week."

Rolf shook all the men's hands as we headed back to our seats. As he put his hand in mine, I felt a piece of paper go in it. I was quick to grab it as I saw a slight smile on his face.

"Well then, I'll leave you to your dinner. *Vi ses.*"

With that, he headed to his table as we went back to our own. I was careful not to glance his way the rest of the night while we enjoyed our food and alcohol but noted when he left the bar. I checked the clock, wanting to wait fifteen minutes before excusing myself for the night. Walrum needed to get back to the facility after all.

CHAPTER TWENTY-FOUR

Nik

"Are you leaving so soon?" I asked as Rebecca nodded to Walrum.

"*Ja*, Alexandra wanted me to get Walrum back to her by eight. We are going to be pushing it already."

I frowned a little. I didn't want her to leave. "You are welcome to come back here after, if you want."

"I don't know, I'm kind of getting tired. I'm not used to drinking this much anymore." She laughed.

Walrum wrapped his arms around her. "Don't worry,

I'll make sure she gets to the base fine." He kissed her on the cheek.

Maybe it was better if they left. I smiled. "Oh, okay. Well, I'll see you tomorrow."

"*Bis dann*," Rebecca said as she waved goodbye.

After they left the bar, I let out the largest breath I ever did hold. Jonathan whistled.

"Damn, that was quite the sigh. You okay?"

"Yeah. Whatever."

"Mmm." Jonathan took a sip of his beer. "Shouldn't you be happy? You have your eyesight back."

"I am. I am."

"That's not the look of someone happy."

I took my beer and downed the rest of it. "Like you said, I just need to wait until all this is over and I can see where the cards end up. If I am lucky, then I get the girl. If I'm not, well, then I'll deal with it when we get there."

"You know, there are probably trillions of other girls out there with at least a few billion with a lot less baggage. And yet here you are, obsessing with the girl with one of the heaviest of bags," Jonathan said as he swayed a little. It was good to know a couple of beers made him honest.

Problem was, he was definitely telling the truth.

I laid my head on the table. "Yeah, I know. But that wants me to protect her even more." I clenched my fist and tapped the table with it. "Just thinking about all the things that Sebastien might have made her do makes me incredibly frustrated. Like, angry beyond belief. I want him dead."

"Don't we all. Because of him, Jacques and I have had to keep our relationship secret for all these years. Although it will never compare to what others have gone through, the loved ones that they have lost. But still, so many years wasted that we could have been together." Jonathan shook his head. "It pissed me off to no end."

"But I suppose all this was worth it to take him down."

"*Oui.*" Jonathan took a drink of his beer. "But the problem is we haven't done that, have we?"

I let out a sigh. "No, we haven't. But you got some information from the two mercenaries?"

"Some, but we aren't sure it's enough. I'll go over it tomorrow. It's loud in here, but you never know."

"Right." I straightened back up. "So you don't trust Walrum with the information?"

Jonathan shrugged. "I'm not sure what to make of him. Something seems off. He seems to remember us, recalls certain missions and things that happened, and he is remembering more and more each day, but then…"

"Then he didn't remember Jason," I finished.

He nodded. "Yeah. I don't know what to make of that. There are stories he referenced that were in this bar. I know that amnesia is strange, and he is still piecing things together, but I don't know. It seemed weird how he reacted."

"I agree." I grabbed one of the remaining fries and munched on it. "And he looked over at Rebecca oddly."

"I noticed that as well. It makes me wonder if this isn't all some setup."

"Setup?"

"I just… I guess I am paranoid. Sebastien has really fucked us up, hasn't he?"

I let out a defeated laugh. "You can say that again. We worked for him that long, and the entire time he had to have known we were sent by Bardon to spy on him. He led us on a wild-goose chase again and again. He played with us like strings on a puppet. Then, after working for him all that time, he sets up to take the fall for that murder."

Jonathan nodded. "He needed us out of the way for something. I wish we could figure out what."

"Or he wanted to experiment on all of us. That's a possibility."

"It is. Or he knew we would escape and wanted to scare us away."

"That could be it."

Jonathan shook his head. "No, if that were the case, he wouldn't have been so focused on getting Rebecca back. I think he just wanted us to suffer."

"Ein stück müll."

"Indeed." He shifted in his seat. "But let's not fret on him. Let's have fun. This is supposed to be a good day —a fun day of you getting your eye back."

I nodded. "Right. Focus on fun. How about a game of darts?"

"Nothing could go wrong there—two guys drinking and sharp objects. Just don't hurt your eye again."

I laughed as we made our way to the board. "One can only hope."

We played darts for a while. Jonathan was a lot better than me, which wasn't a surprise as he had always been skilled at this game. Rebecca was too and usually would beat Jonathan. I didn't have any skill for the game. Nor the other games. Nor most things, as she was good at anything she put her mind to.

I threw one of the darts and hit a bull's-eye. I pumped my fists up in victory. "There! I did it! We can all go home now!"

Jonathan laughed as he slapped my back. "You do realize I beat you even with that bull's-eye, right?"

"Yup."

"Then yes, we should probably head back. Jonathan didn't want me staying out too late."

"You will have a nice warm bed to go back to. Meanwhile, I'll just have to head back. All alone."

Jonathan sighed. "You can come back with me, if you want."

"I'm not having some weird threesome."

"No, Jesus, I mean come back and have some coffee or something. *Pour l'amour de Dieu.*"

"*Entschuldigen.* Yeah, that sounds nice. Then I'll leave you two alone."

He patted my back again as we said goodbye to Jason and left the bar for the night. Jonathan and I stumbled around a little even though I swore I was sobering up after that game of darts. Perhaps I was mistaken—

perhaps I didn't hit the bull's-eye but my eyes deceived me. I just hoped I didn't put a hole in the wall. Again.

"Nice night out," I commented as I stared up at the stars. "It's cool but not too cold."

"*Oui*, too bad during the day it's so humid."

"Whose idea was it to put a military base here?"

"They want to make sure we are fit for any type of weather, so they pick the worst places."

"That seems like it's accurate."

"I know it is. Jacques told me it long ago."

It didn't seem like any of the bases were in nice areas. It sucked. I couldn't imagine having to live here all my life, even though I practically had. But I knew someday I could leave to find a nice place.

I commented, "It's weird so many people live here as well. I mean, there's a huge city."

"Humans are stupid and build stuff where they know they will hate it if they go outside. That way they think it's better to stay inside and work more."

I thought about that for a moment. "Huh. That's an odd way of putting it."

He shrugged. "That's just what I imagine."

"Well, whatever the reason, they are idiots."

"Agreed."

"And yet you picked to stay here after this is all over."

"I have to. My *mon amour* is an admiral. I'll probably have to live here for quite some time until he retires at least."

"Do you think he will?"

"Eventually. But not for awhile. He likes his job, I guess."

"And you?" I asked. "Do you like being here?"

"I like my job, yes. I mean, I don't know what else I would do at this point. Almost forty and all that."

"Ugh, don't remind me. I did not expect to be here when I was forty."

"Well, hopefully you'll be out of here before then."

"Damn straight."

We made it to the entrance to the base. We scanned in our badges and stepped inside. It was quiet, as most were already in bed due to their curfew. I hiccupped as we made our way to Admiral Bardon and Jonathan's room. I just prayed I wouldn't walk in on him waiting for Jonathan or something. I might vomit if that was the case. Because he was still a dad figure to me.

Jonathan knocked on the door. "*Mon ami*, I am back."

The door slid open, and Bardon was at his desk, staring at some screens. Apparently, all he did was work. That did not surprise me one bit. He glanced at the clock.

"You got back a bit earlier than I expected."

Jonathan shrugged. "I promised this boy some coffee."

"Ah. Well, sit down. I'll make you some."

I took a seat. "Too much work at the office?"

Bardon sighed. "Always. I'm just going through the report for what those two mercenaries told us. They gave us a name, but the more I search, the less I find, I swear."

"Did they give a fake name?"

"It's possible, but even then, I should have some clue. I also was able to trace back the money they were given to someone in the YamaXie Nation, but that led nowhere."

"So whoever it was has ties," I said as he handed me the coffee.

"Sebastien has a lot of ties, yes. He has been weaving this web for a couple of decades. I am not sure this trial is going to land. And if he gets out…"

"He's coming after our heads. Got it." I sipped the

coffee. It was bitter but hit the spot.

"We need this to work," Bardon said. "Whatever the cost."

I nodded. That was the understatement of the century.

CHAPTER TWENTY-FIVE

Rebecca

"You didn't say anything about that bartender."

I sighed. I knew Walrum was going to interrogate me about that later. "I didn't realize he was still working there. I didn't think it was important. You pulled it off fine—they won't suspect anything."

"As long as you know Nik's life is on the line."

"I know. I know."

We kept on walking. We didn't have much to say to each other, which made it all the more awkward. I couldn't wait to get back, especially since I knew what was waiting for me.

Checking in at the entrance, we made our way to the facility that Walrum stayed in. As we approached, Walrum turned to me.

"You have everything ready, correct? The trial is in two weeks."

I narrowed my eyes. "Everything I need to be doing I have been doing. I contacted those mercenaries for him, although they weren't supposed to try to kill us. That was against what he promised."

"Well, you made it out alive, so no harm done."

"Easy for you to say. You weren't there."

Walrum laughed as we entered the facility. I checked him into the front desk and kissed him good night like a fiancée would. The moment I stepped outside, I wiped my mouth, wanting to spit. That would have been obvious.

Taking the paper out of my pocket, I checked it over. Apparently, Rolf was stationed in the admiral quarters. I would have to be careful not to be spotted by Bardon. He was likely still at work or already retired for the evening. It would just be the morning I would have to be the most careful about.

It was past curfew for the cadets, so there wasn't anyone wandering about this late. I took in the nice night air and let out a long breath. So far everything had been going according to plan. I didn't want to think of what the outcome would be. That is, if I actually went along with Sebastien's plan. I was still trying to figure out a way to outsmart him. So far, I had nothing.

But that would be tomorrow's problem. Tonight, I was just focusing on one thing and one thing only.

I knocked on his door, and it swung open. He stood there in the doorway, shirtless. Even though he was about the same age as Sebastien and Bardon, he was still a bit muscular. He, of course, wasn't as athletic as Nik, but one could tell he kept up some of his military training.

"Well, that didn't take long. I thought you would hang out with your friends a little longer. I was just about to hit the shower. Care to join?"

I could feel my face warm. "I could use a shower."

I stepped inside, and the door slid behind me. He turned to head to the bathroom as I pulled my tank off and followed him. He started the water and turned to me with a slight smile.

"You know, I didn't think I would ever get to hear

from you again. Not after that whole ordeal on Nash Mir." He began taking his belt off and pulling off his trousers.

Shrugging, I pulled off my sports bra and stripped. "You know how things go—mess with Sebastien, get screwed over."

He laughed. "So it was him who set you all up. I had my suspicion."

"Well, we have no proof."

"But if we are being honest, right?" He smiled as he took off his boxers. I bit my lip as he was already ready for this. I pulled off my own black underwear and followed him into the shower.

The water was a perfect temperature—not too hot that it was scalding but hot enough to relax my muscles. Rolf didn't hesitate as he wrapped his arms around me and pulled me in close under the showerhead. His lips met mine, tasting still of the whiskey I had seen him drink earlier that night. My hands ran across his wet chest as I twirled some of the hair with my fingers. His own hands slipped down my back and cupped my bare ass. I let out a moan as he pulled me close.

His lips moved away from mine as he whispered in my ear, "How long has it been?"

"Too long, to be honest. Probably five or six years."

"Right before you and Walrum started going out."

"Yeah, that sounds about right."

"I always gave you my room number when I saw you."

"I wasn't going to cheat on him, and you knew that."

"Is it cheating if it's no strings attached?" he asked as he lifted me up and gently lowered my hips down his torso and onto him. I helped get his member inside me with my hands. I let out a moan.

"Quick to go all the way, I see," I commented as I wrapped my legs around his waist and arms around the back of his neck.

"Don't worry, we will have more time to play. I just don't want to waste too much water."

He moved his lips back against mine as he shoved my body against the cool wall of the shower. I moved my hips as he moved against me, pushing me harder and harder against the wall. Although a little bit uncomfortable, the slight pain of it all made it that much better. I knew it was wrong for me to feel that way, but after everything I had been through, my belief was that it made me feel alive.

I bit at his lip as he pounded me harder and harder,

tugging his lip a bit as I could feel waves of pleasure start coming. I let out a moan as I felt it all come at once. I squeezed him tighter, not wanting it to leave me as I could feel every nerve in my body give way. Rolf pulled my hips in as tight as he could, breathing as heavily as I was. I leaned my head against his shoulder, water still pouring down on us. My body was tingling now, coming down from the height that was this orgasm.

He whispered in my ear, "Don't worry, *min kære*, the night is just getting started."

After the shower, Rolf poured us both a glass of wine. I sat at the table, wearing nothing but one of his shirts, and sipped on it.

"It's a pinot noir, made all the way in Nouveau Départ. Hard to get your hands on, let alone imported to this planet."

It was sweet with light fruity flavors. I had to admit, it was rather smooth. "And you are wasting it on me?"

"It's not wasting it if I am serving it to my favorite *kvinde*."

I raised an eyebrow. "Favorite? I thought you always said no strings attached."

"And none are. But you are still my favorite booty call."

I raised a glass to him. "Likewise. And I'll be honest, you are my favorite admiral to fuck."

He raised his glass and met mine. "I can toast to that. I'm glad to know I'm a better lover than Sebastien."

I made a face and took a large gulp. Rolf took a sip of his own and nodded to me. "Don't drink it out of anger. Enjoy it."

"Are you talking about the wine or yourself?"

He let out a laugh. "Both, I guess." He set his glass down and leaned back. "So, tell me, what were the past three years like for you?"

I raised an eyebrow. "Really? Are you going to go all therapist on me now? I should report you."

He waved that idea off. "You were never officially my patient and we're two grown adults. I doubt even you could damage my reputation. Even Sebastien has tried and failed."

"I'm surprised you are alive, although I don't think he ever found out about our trysts after we broke up."

"And before the two of you were an item, if I recall correctly." He grinned a little.

"Right, I forgot about that night."

He clutched his chest. "Oh, you wound me so."

"Stop being dramatic. Life has been a complete mess for me."

"If you went back to graduation, would you decline Sebastien's offer then?"

"In a heartbeat."

"Even if it meant never meeting Nik?"

I let out a laugh. "How did you know?"

"Because I know you, Rebecca. I know how you think, and I know the two of you have traveled together for the past three years." He nodded toward his tablet. "Also, because Bardon forwarded me everything you have talked about so far."

I frowned. "So, I am a patient?"

He shrugged. "Not technically yet." He leaned forward. "So, anything you want to talk to me about?"

"*Nein*. I just came here to fuck."

Standing up, he stepped behind me. He kissed the side of my cheek. "Not to confess 'oh, I'm still working for Sebastien, please save me'?"

I turned to him. "I could confess that, but then I would have to kill you."

He kissed my lips. "I miss that sass of yours."

"And I miss that sadistic sarcasm of yours."

"In another life, we would have made a great team."

"In another life, I wouldn't be as fucked-up as I am now."

"That is true. And you would be a lot less fun." He kissed me again, this time a little deeper. He moved away and sat back down across from me. "But I am interested, why did you keep moving around when you were in hiding? I wouldn't think you would be found that easily."

"You know why I had to keep moving—Sebastien has men everywhere and was looking for me."

"Are you sure of that?"

"I overheard him when his little minions communicated with him more than once, *ja*."

He scratched his chin. I raised an eyebrow. "What is it?"

"It's nothing. Just a thought occurred to me. You are definitely his weak spot in that sense. He wouldn't put so much effort on anyone else."

"Anyone else would be caught or killed a lot easier than me."

"That is most definitely true. But I suppose that talk is for another time." He took his glass and took a large gulp, finishing his drink. "Shall we pick up where we left off?"

CHAPTER TWENTY-SIX

Nik

A couple of days had passed since our outing. Jørgensen was making rounds, talking to those we brought in from the facility when we'd captured Sebastien, along with the two mercenaries. He wasn't able to get any more information out of them than we were able to, unfortunately.

But the time was coming when he needed to interrogate Sebastien. Bardon had requested that we all be present for that day—to make sure he didn't miss anything—but I had a feeling it was partially to see what Rebecca's reaction waould be. So far, she hadn't seen Sebastien since we arrived there, and I couldn't blame her. She tried to kill him the last time she was with him due to what he did to Walrum. But now he was improving, and she was off the drugs she had been taking. Overall, she seemed to be doing better.

We entered the viewing room. Sebastien wasn't in the interrogation room, which was somewhat a relief. I needed to mentally prepare myself to see him more. I glanced at Rebecca, who was biting at her nails—something she only did when incredibly nervous. I gave her a half-hearted smile, trying to reassure her I was there if anything happened. She smiled back as the door opened.

I held my breath as Sebastien stepped in. He was wearing a standard shirt and dark pants that are issued to all the inmates, although because he was an admiral and because everyone was afraid of him, I had a feeling he got better treatment. His wrists were bound in front of him as he was taken to the chair and table. The guard ushered him over and linked the cuffs to the table so he couldn't attack or escape. The entire time, Sebastien grinned as if he were simply playing some game. He thanked the guard as he walked to the door.

"What a fucking psychopath," Jonathan whispered as he crossed his arms.

Bardon nodded in agreement. "He has had that grin the entire time he has been in there. It's frightening, to say the least."

"Where's Admiral Dr. Jørgensen?" I asked. "Shouldn't he be here by now?"

Rebecca answered. "Sebastien hates waiting, so Jørgensen is trying to tick him off a bit before their exchange, hoping to bring something out of him." She glanced over to me and shrugged. "At least that's my guess."

That made sense. He really did hate waiting, which was interesting since he had been weaving webs for such a long time. I supposed waiting and patience could be two different things.

Ten minutes passed as Sebastien sat in the room. He didn't speak or ask for anything but just grinned devilishly as he peered forward. I wanted to smack the look off his face, but at that point I couldn't. Rebecca kept her arms folded as she stared at the bound man. I couldn't read her at that moment, but it seemed to me a lot was going through her mind.

But it didn't seem he was fazed by the wait. The door finally opened, and Jørgensen stepped inside.

"Sorry to keep you waiting, Admiral Wilde. I got tied up with some other matters."

The corner of Sebastien's mouth twitched. Apparently, he was affected by it. "I am sure you did."

Jørgensen took a seat across from Sebastien and pulled out his tablets, setting them up so he could go through the questions he'd already made and make any notes he deemed important.

"Now, where shall we begin?"

Sebastien shrugged. "You tell me, Admiral. You are the specialist after all."

"I guess we shall start with your father. He was an admiral before you, isn't that correct? He was the reason you got so far in the military."

Rebecca let out a laugh of a breath. Jørgensen was definitely good at what he did.

Sebastien blinked a couple of times as he opened his mouth. "I got to where I am by my own merit. He and I didn't get along as others might have thought."

"Oh? I had seen you two interact before his passing. He seemed to be quite fond of you."

"We made good appearances, but he didn't want

anything to do with me. I had to earn my own way. As you and everyone else knows, I trained under a different admiral."

"Right. That is my mistake then. I just figured since your father and Admiral Müller were good friends, he might have pulled some strings."

"My father was good friends with everyone in the military. He kissed up to everyone."

"Except you?"

Sebastien let out a laugh. "He only kissed up to people he thought would benefit him. He never saw me as a benefit."

"He sounds like he is the complete opposite then. He used kind words and friendship to get what he wanted, and you use fear."

"My father never got what he wanted. He might have been an admiral, but everyone walked all over him because of his friendliness."

"So you see friendliness as a weakness?"

Sebastien's smile turned into a slight frown. "You know that I hate you, right? You are one of the few people I despise the most."

Jørgensen jotted down some notes. "Oh, I know. The feeling is mutual. You have done horrible, monstrous things, and I would like to see you behind bars."

His grin was back. "You have no proof."

"In due time, Admiral. Your claws aren't as deep as you think. Everyone makes mistakes. You are no exception."

"I can't wait to see what false evidence you find. It will be like a magic show."

Jørgensen ignored him as he tapped on the screen a bit more. "Tell me about your captains."

"Those traitors to our nation? What about them?"

"Do you honestly think that the men you trained and were under your care murdered out of cold blood?"

"Have you met them? I have no doubt they did. And yet Admiral Bardon went behind my back and reinstated them. I never gave permission for that."

I rolled my eyes. Jonathan leaned over to whisper in my ear. "Can we just kill him now?"

"I'll cover you, if you want."

"I wouldn't mind at this point. I'm sick of his lies."

"Don't worry, *messieurs*, he will be taken down. I promise."

"Except Rebecca, right? You reinstated her before Admiral Bardon got the chance."

Sebastien's lip twitched. "That's right. I know she

wasn't a part of it all. She was my best captain."

"But she was there with them, wasn't she? What makes you think she was innocent?"

His eyes flickered to the one-way mirror, straight at Rebecca. It was creepy that he was able to tell that she was there. I watched as Rebecca clenched her fists.

"Because she wouldn't disobey orders."

Even that comment sent shivers down my spine. I watched as Rebecca's eyes narrowed. I wanted to tell her it was fine and that he couldn't hurt her anymore, but I wasn't sure that could even be a guarantee. I had a feeling his goal at that point was for all our heads.

"I see. She is quite loyal then?"

"Quite. I wish I could have found her earlier to tell her that she was cleared of those crimes her colleagues had done, but she is quite clever."

Jørgensen typed some more things on his tablet. "If I recall correctly, she performed more missions under you than the others."

"Yes, she is a bit younger than them, so I wanted to teach her the ropes myself."

I felt as if my heart had sunk into my stomach. I didn't like how he said that nor where this was going. Even Rebecca appeared as if she were going to vomit.

Glancing over to Bardon, I found him and Jonathan exchanging glances.

"It seemed to me you kept her to yourself far beyond what was needed to show her the ropes. Perhaps I am mistaken, but were you two lovers?"

Sebastien leaned back a little, let out a laugh. He narrowed his eyes to Jørgensen, who kept the same stoic expression he always did.

I stared at Rebecca, who was turning white as if she had seen a ghost. Bardon and Jonathan had said that her and Sebastien's relationship was deeper than what they led on, but I couldn't actually believe them. But now…

"What are you trying to get at, Admiral Dr. Jørgensen? Hmm? You want me to say yes, that she's my little secret? That she is and always has been precious to me? As if that is wrong?" He pointed at the one-way mirror. "Meanwhile, one of my captains has been sleeping with Admiral Bardon? As if I didn't know?"

"It was just a question—apparently a question that has hit a chord."

Rebecca whispered to herself, "I think I'm going to be sick."

"Well, I am a little sensitive. See, she left me for one

of her comrades. I was a little heartbroken. Especially since after all the time we'd spent together, to find she was having an affair with Walrum hurt me in ways she could never imagine."

Rebecca was shaking her head now. She opened her mouth, but no words came out. She looked like she was ready to run away from there. I couldn't blame her. I knew he was lying through his teeth, but I wondered how much of it was true.

Jørgensen tapped his finger on his tablet and cocked his head to the side. "Funny. That's not what she told me the other night."

I didn't like how Jørgensen said that. The other night? Rebecca took a step back, as if she were ready to go in there and beat both the admirals into a pulp. What exactly happened the other night? And where was Jørgensen going with that?

CHAPTER TWENTY-SEVEN

Rebecca

I was ready to go in there and kill them both. Did they have no morals? Wasn't there some law that a therapist couldn't mention what was said in confidence to them? *Scheiße*, this was not going to go well—not with how Sebastien's eyes narrowed and his once cocky smile gone from his face.

"Excuse me?"

"Well, from my recollection, you two had a big fight because you, Admiral Wilde, cheated on her quite a few years back. Rebecca had no one to turn to, you see." Jørgensen licked his lips—lips I knew I wouldn't be kissing ever again after the stunt he was pulling. "So I was the one who comforted her. Then, of course, one thing led to another."

I couldn't move. I felt as if I were frozen in place. This was going to end horribly. Sebastien was going to kill him. There was no doubt in my mind.

Walrum commented, "So who haven't you fucked?"

I ignored him. It was a good percentage of the men in this room and in the room that we were watching. That wasn't many, but it sure felt like it at that moment—especially since they were all standing there. I didn't want to turn to Nik and see the hurt on his face—especially since I knew what was going to come next.

Sebastien was trying to keep his cool, but it was apparent on his face that he was going to lose it. After these two weeks, this was going to be the reason he snapped. I had to hand it to Jørgensen, he knew how to get under his skin. But I was still pissed.

"You did what?"

"Let me be clear—neither of us have feelings for

each other, but I have to admit, she is one of my favorite persons to rendezvous with. I can always expect a good time with her.”

Sebastien was turning red. Fuck.

“Wh—” He smiled and laughed a little. “When was this again?”

Fuck.

“Well, we first met… It’s been a while. I think she just graduated. Maybe a year or so later we hit it off and had a one-night stand. Then we ran into each other a few times after that through the years. Then about seven years back we hooked up. She was drinking her sorrows away. Something about walking in on you fucking another girl? Then, of course, this week.” Jørgensen gave him a grin.

“You— Heh.” Sebastien glanced down at the ground, as if trying to calculate what to do next. “That *Zicke*.”

“She was never in a relationship when we had our meetings. Seems to me you were sleeping around the entire time you were together. You are the one who destroyed your relationship.”

“I love her! I’ll always love her! She is mine and mine alone! None of those other girls meant anything.”

Gott, I was going to throw up or murder someone. It

could go either way. Especially since I knew Sebastien was on the brink of breaking.

Jørgensen shrugged. "The two of us don't mean anything to each other either. So, what's the difference?"

"The difference?" Sebastien stood up. The guard went to make him go back in his chair, but Jørgensen gestured to leave him alone. "The difference is that I made her into who she is! I trained her! I took her on all my missions! I trusted her with everything!"

"You trusted her with all your missions?"

"Yes! She was there! She was always there! If you are going to arrest me for treason and war crimes, then she should be right here with me!"

"So, you are admitting you did perform treason and war crimes?"

"Yes! I did! I have killed countless people! I was behind all the experiments! I have kidnapped and murdered countless scientists!" He pointed at the mirror —straight at me. "And she was there, at my side! She was the one I had murder them! She was the one who was right there at my side where she belongs!"

I didn't even wait for the door to swing open behind me—I raised my hands and began to get down on my knees. Seconds later guards came, guns pointed straight at me.

"Captain Rebecca Kompen, you are to be taken into custody for further questioning," one of the guards barked down at me.

No one in the room protested—still in shock with what Jørgensen was able to get out of Sebastien. I wanted to laugh and cry at the same time. I glanced up at Bardon, who was frowning as if he were trying to solve this mess. I had told him Sebastien would take me down with him—I guess he really thought differently. Whatever, this didn't change much—at least not for the plan I had already put in motion.

Because everything Jørgensen had said was according to plan. Granted, I was still pissed he went through with it, but I had known he was going to do anything he could to get Sebastien to talk. Now we would have to figure out the next step.

I couldn't look at Nik, knowing he was disappointed in me. I kept my head down as the guards pulled me up and bound my wrists behind my back. They pushed me out the door and to my own cell.

I just really hoped they wouldn't put me in the same

room as Sebastien. I just could not deal with that at the moment. I wasn't sure if I would try to kill him or vice versa. He appeared a little upset. Just a little.

Hopefully Nik would be fine. Sebastien wanted to teach me a lesson at the moment—the lesson that only he could have affairs but I had to be completely loyal to just him. I wanted to vomit. I had spent six years of my life as his plaything—six years that should have been the best part of my life, but instead I was involved with a psychopath. A psychopath who was able to get me to do unspeakable things. I didn't deserve to be cleared of those sins even if Sebastien had tricked me over the years—slowly grooming me so I didn't ask questions.

I should have known better.

But I was young and naive and honestly thought that he cared about me. But alas, here I was, in a prison cell, my sins finally caught up with me.

For now, at least.

The door opened, and a guard stepped in. "You have a visitor."

I raised an eyebrow. "Oh? So soon?"

I was surprised to find who stepped in—it was Alexandra. I guess it was coming sooner or later.

She only took a few steps inside when she stopped

and stared at me.

"It was you that night, wasn't it?" she asked.

I sighed. "This again?"

"Yes. This again. You killed my parents, didn't you?"

I slowly nodded. There was no point in keeping secrets now. My life was fucked.

"And you saw me that night, hiding."

I nodded again. She folded her arms.

"Why did you save me?"

I let out a laugh. "I'm not going to kill some kid."

"You didn't tell Admiral Wilde that I was there, did you?"

"*Nein.* He would have made me kill you. No witnesses and all that."

"But you let me live."

"*Ja,* you were a kid. Even I have morals, little they may be."

I glanced up at her. Her eyes were filled with tears as different emotions ran across her face.

"I'll never forgive you for what you did."

"I don't expect anyone to forgive me. I committed horrible crimes."

"Let me finish. I won't forgive you, but thank you for not killing me. It forced me to be here and be of help to take that monster down. You had a choice that night."

"The right choice would have been killing Sebastien a long time ago. But alas, here we are. And here I am."

She turned and left me sitting there. That girl made no sense, but her comment put a smile to my lips.

Now I just had to make the right choice once more.

CHAPTER TWENTY-EIGHT

Nik

"This is ludicrous, and you know it."

I slammed my hands on Bardon's desk. He held up his hand.

"Calm down, Nik. She isn't on trial yet; everything is still getting sorted out."

"But Sebastien said she was there with him on all those missions. That can't be possible, can it? Would she have kept quiet about that this whole time?" I asked.

Jonathan, who was behind Bardon, leaned against the frame of the window. "Would you tell someone of all the crimes you had committed if it meant that you were going to go to jail as well?"

That was a fair point. "But... I can't believe she would murder people for him."

Bardon leaned back. "Nik, I don't know how to tell you this, but everything he said is true."

I frowned. "How do you know that?"

"Because she has been meeting with me every day for the past couple of weeks, confessing. That USB that she found is mostly evidence against her as well as Sebastien. I didn't think we were going to be able to use it because it would have marked her guilty as well. But it seems Jørgensen was able to get Sebastien to confess by pushing his buttons dealing with her. Now we have no choice but to submit it as evidence."

I leaned back and stared up at the ceiling. I couldn't believe what he had said—and how he was able to push Sebastien's buttons like that. It was sick he used her the way that he did, but it had been successful. But also, I was pissed she went and slept with him earlier that week. What was going through her mind? I guess I couldn't blame her in the long run. She and I weren't dating. But what about Walrum?

Tilting my head forward, I asked, "So what does that mean for Rebecca? Will she be sentenced for life? Or given the death penalty?"

Bardon shook his head. "No, I won't allow them to do that. But she will probably be sentenced a few years, a decade maybe. I'll try to do my best to see if she confesses, if the jury will let her go free."

"But then anyone who is pro-Sebastien will try to murder her for confessing," Jonathan added. "So I think, right now, she is royally screwed."

I shook my head. This couldn't be happening—after everything, this could not be happening.

"What about Walrum?" I asked. "Do you think he is actually healing or that this is some complex plot with him?"

Bardon shrugged. "At this point, we can't be certain. That is why I am not trusting him with any important intel. However, as we have already seen, Sebastien has spies everywhere. I don't think he is that high risk in comparison."

He had a point there. It was unbelievable that so

many people were still on his side. Even from a cell, he had everyone stepping on glass.

"So, since he has confessed, is the trial going to be rushed?"

Bardon nodded. "Yes. It will be in three days, including the video of his confession. Rebecca will have to be questioned soon if she wants to get some kind of relief."

I sighed. This really couldn't be happening. "May I be there when she does?"

Bardon examined me for a moment. "You may, but you can't be in the room she is in. You have to stay in the viewing room."

"Yeah, I know."

Jonathan nodded at me. "You know, you are the only reason she hasn't confessed. If she didn't want you to think he was a monster, she probably would have come forward long ago."

"Great. That makes me feel oh so much better."

Bardon leaned forward. "What he's trying to say is that she cares about you. So stop being so sad, wondering what her feelings are for you if she didn't even tell you the truth."

I frowned a little, but they had a point. I doubt

Rebecca even knew how to trust anyone after what Sebastien had done to her. I doubted Walrum even knew the truth, as he was working for Bardon and would have reported it.

"Can I see the photos?" I asked.

Bardon hesitated but realized I would see them sooner or later. "*Oui.*"

He pulled out his tablet and plugged in the USB. After a few moments, he turned the tablet to me.

I grabbed it, staring at the photo of Rebecca as she held her gun up to the back of someone's head. We had killed many criminals through the years, but this was different. She had a cold look in her eyes, as if she were trying to turn off all emotions she had.

I flipped the next photo. Many were the same—her assassinating someone with Sebastien standing right there. A couple of them had him kissing her on the cheek. I flipped through more and more photos when finally, one was at one of Sebastien's facilities.

My eyes widened. It was grotesque—people were strapped down and opened up as doctors performed procedures. And there, in the back, was Rebecca, standing shoulder to shoulder with Sebastien.

There was no way those were real. I couldn't believe

it.

Bardon took the tablet back. "I'm sorry, Nik. I doubt she had a choice. I have been trying everything I could to keep her safe, but it did not work."

"So I take it you believe in her too?" I asked.

Bardon nodded. "I know that Sebastien is good at grooming people. He gets people in a position where they can't say no. So yes, I think she is more innocent than she will accept. As are many others."

I bit my lip. "The next few days are going to be crucial. Do you have any idea of what we should do?"

"Well," he began as he brought his hands together. "I have a thought."

CHAPTER TWENTY-NINE

Rebecca

It was almost dinner time, and I wondered if they were going to bring me food I would actually eat. It wasn't like I was in a position where I could really complain or order different foods, but I didn't know if I could stomach meat of any kind. Just the thought of it was making my stomach hurt. That and everything that was going on and had happened over the years. I didn't want to rehash those memories, and yet that was what I kept doing all this time.

I really wanted to take a vial of morphine-B.

Not only did it make me calm down in situations like this, but it also helped the shaking, which I was experiencing. I kept moving, hoping that whoever was watching me wouldn't notice what was going on with my body. All I needed again was an embarrassing visit to the hospital.

I was better than this—I was better than him. I didn't need a drug to get control over my mind again. I was in control, not him.

The more I kept telling myself that, the more I knew I was lying. He had made his way into my mind long ago —how else would he have gotten me to do all those things? If he wasn't inside my head, then that would mean I was the monster, and there was no way I could accept that. No—I was not a monster. He was. I was just a puppet.

His stupid little *Puppe*.

The door opened, and I expected it to be a guard with my meal that I wasn't going to eat, but I was wrong. It was Nik.

Damn. I had hoped that he wouldn't come by here. I had hoped I completely crushed him so that I would never have to face him again. I sat down on the bed.

I looked away as he brought my tray of food inside. He set it on the table.

"I figured they wouldn't get you the food you wanted, so I brought some myself," he said calmly.

"Danke."

He stood there a moment, staring down at the plate. We didn't say a word to each other, but I could feel the tension growing. My arms were shaking even more now, and I took long, deep breaths.

"You know I love you, right?"

Tears already made their way to my eyes. "Yes. That is why I could never tell you the truth."

"I would have helped you—we could have come back earlier and got Bardon's help."

I shook my head. "He had men everywhere. You have no idea how many of them I took down during those three years. If we had set one foot into the Nreff Nation, he would have gotten me straightaway—just like he did."

He was quiet for a moment, as if he knew that as well. "I would have helped any way that I could."

"And he would have killed you. Just like he did Walrum."

More silence. I glanced away, wondering what there

was to say. It felt like all the words in the languages I knew were gone. There was nothing I could say.

He took a seat next to me on the bed. We sat there for a few moments, just wanting to be next to each other, knowing nothing could make this better. I wanted to tell him everything—I wanted to tell him how sorry I was and how I was a monster who didn't deserve his love, but I had no idea where to start. Instead, I just stared down at the ground. My lies had been for his sake. He knew that, but there still was so much more he didn't know.

"Bardon is going to try to get you some leniency if you confess to everything. I think you'll be taken in tomorrow, so think about that."

I nodded. "I will. But honestly, that isn't going to do any good."

"He thinks you would only have to be in jail for a few years, ten at most."

That wasn't the problem—the problem was what was going to happen at the trial. I still had no idea how I was going to fix it all, but I had a few things in motion. I just had to pray that they would work.

"Is he going to use those photos then?" I asked.

Nik slowly nodded. "Yeah. He will."

"Hopefully the fact that I didn't destroy them right away works in my favor. I mean, all of them had me in it as well. I figured they would, but I didn't need anyone blaming me for what happened out there. It doesn't matter now though. Bastien confessed, adding my name to his list. Just because I fucked Admiral Jørgensen." I let out a laugh. "Of all the things."

"He shouldn't have used you like that. It was unprofessional."

"He used any means necessary. We knew that would be the only way to take Sebastien out. I don't blame him, although I might slap him the next time I see him, given the chance at least."

"I'll pull a few strings and see if I can get that to happen."

I chuckled. "*Danke*. I would appreciate that."

A few moments passed when he stood up. "I should probably get going. I still have a lot to get ready for the trial."

"Right," I whispered. "*Viel Glück*. I'll be here."

"Hope you enjoy your food."

With that he left me. After wiping the tears off my face, I got up to check what he brought in for me. It was some pasta with tomato sauce. I picked at it, trying to eat as much as I could, even though my stomach hurt beyond belief.

Why could nothing go according to plan?

CHAPTER THIRTY

Nik

I stood with Jonathan and Bardon as Rebecca was brought into the interrogation room. I could see her arms shaking, even though she was trying to keep a brave face for all those who were watching. I wished I could comfort her and tell her that everything was going to be all right. But honestly? I doubted it was going to be. We were all knee-deep in this *Scheiße*.

After a few moments, Admiral Dr. Jørgensen stepped inside. I turned to Bardon.

"Really? He's going to be the one questioning her?"

Bardon shrugged. "He's the best at what he does."

Rebecca yanked on the cuffs that were chained on the table. "*Verdammt*. I was hoping I could slip out of these and punch you a few times."

"I'm sorry for betraying your trust, Rebecca, but you knew it had to be done for the good of this trial."

"Easy for you to say—you aren't the one in cuffs."

Jørgensen let out a little laugh. "That's fair. But I am truly here to help. Depending on what information you give us now, we will be able to cut your sentence down to two to three years. You understand?"

She nodded. "*Ja*."

"All right." He took a seat and pulled out his tablets. "Let's start from the beginning. You began serving under Admiral Wilde when you were seventeen?"

Rebecca nodded. "That's right. Fifteen years ago."

Damn, had that much time gone by? I couldn't believe it.

"And you began relations with Admiral Wilde?"

Her eyes narrowed at him. "Two years into my service."

"Was that when he started taking you on his missions with him?"

She shook her head. "No, that was gradual. First it was something like just capturing someone that I was told was a criminal. Then it escalated more and more each time until I was in too deep to get out."

Jørgensen made some notes. "What about after the two of you had split?"

"He still made me go on those missions. He always tried to get close to me, and I pushed him away. He never forced anything physically, but… disobeying him always came at a cost. Perhaps I would be captured by an enemy as they miraculously had my location, or let's say, set up for murder?"

"So you are saying he set the four of you up for the murder of the representative of Nash Mir?"

She nodded. "Yes."

"Because he found out about the mission against him?"

Rebecca shook her head. "He always knew that Nik, Walrum, and Jonathan were spying on him. That was why he had hired them. No, he set that up so he could kill Walrum, or I guess mess with his brain, because the two of us were engaged."

My jaw dropped. What? I couldn't believe that. First off, was Sebastien really that devious to keep us near so he knew what we were up to? And then, after all that, to get so selfish that he tried to kill Walrum like that?

Then again, after seeing how he reacted yesterday, I couldn't see how it would be a lie. He had really done all this just to take his revenge on Rebecca. I felt sick to my stomach. All this time, and this is what she had been dealing with. No wonder she didn't trust anyone.

"Do you have proof of that?" Jørgensen asked.

She shook her head. "Unfortunately no, but we have Walrum, and he's beginning to remember that day more and more. Perhaps questioning him again will bring back what possible things Sebastien had said to him. He said plenty when I was with him right before he was arrested."

I bit my lip. I couldn't imagine what she had gone through with the mission just weeks ago—how much agony it caused. It was no wonder she kept taking that morphine, not wanting to have that escape. If I were her, I would have never been able to get off it either.

"Can you give us more names and locations of facilities? Whether those people are dead or those places cleaned up?" Jørgensen asked, handing him the tablet. "Write them all down."

"Including the ones I murdered, you mean?"

He nodded. "Everything you can remember."

Rebecca did just that. The more she typed, the more my stomach ached. Sure, we all had killed a lot of people—but for us it had been kill or be killed, or we were taking down an enemy of the state. I can't imagine what she had felt when it occurred to her that people she was ordered to destroy were innocent.

As she typed, Bardon turned to Jonathan and me. "This is going to take a while. Jonathan, will you go check with Alexandra to see if Walrum is available to be questioned?"

Jonathan nodded and left us.

"What do you want me to do?" I asked. I didn't like being there—especially since I couldn't do anything to help Rebecca.

"How are your hackings skills, Nik?"

I raised an eyebrow, not sure how much I should let on since I wasn't a hacker when I was in the military—I had picked it up when we were on the run. "They are fairly good?"

"Are you lying?"

I let out a laugh. "Fine. They are great. What did you have in mind?"

Bardon bit his lip. "It is going to be complicated, but

Rebecca has something she isn't telling us. She is giving us all this information easier than she would have in the past. It seems to me she is being ordered to do it. I want you to bypass the security system so it shows a loop of her sleeping tonight. Then we are going to go in and talk to her. I'll place guards that I trust outside her door and cause some other problems that will take the focus off her. Can you do that for me?"

I nodded. "What do you think she is hiding?"

Bardon shrugged. "I'm not sure. But between the three of us and Admiral Dr. Jørgensen, I think we will be able to figure it out."

CHAPTER THIRTY-ONE

Rebecca

It felt as if something was around my throat. I couldn't breathe—I couldn't do anything but gasp for air, but nothing was coming in.

"You are mine and mine alone!"

My eyes opened, and I saw a figure standing over me. I grabbed whoever it was by the collar and pulled him down, rolling on top of him, ready to punch them.

"*Mon Dieu!* Rebecca, it's us!"

My eyes focused more, and I was able to see it was

Jonathan. There was still some light in this room—I should have been able to see him, but I had been in such a daze with my adrenaline pumping.

I got off him but didn't apologize. I turned to find Nik and Rolf standing there as well.

"See," Rolf began as he gestured to Jonathan. "That's why Nik and I didn't wake her. We know better than to mess with her while she's sleeping."

Nik nodded in agreement, although he seemed a bit awkward.

"What are you all doing here?"

"We have fifteen minutes before Bardon's distraction is over," Rolf explained. "So that is how much time you have to tell us what is really going on here."

I smiled. So Rolf and Bardon understood me as well as I had hoped. I crossed my arms. "If this fails, you do realize we all die, right? Brutally murdered. I mean, I probably won't be. I'll just have to watch."

"Just hurry, okay? I feel it's a bit more complicated than what you'll be able to give us," Rolf said.

I nodded. "You are right. It's Sebastien after all." I let out a sigh, wondering where to start. "When I was captured or whatever by Sebastien and he took me to the facility, he gave me his plan. I had to follow it carefully or Nik would be killed."

"What about me?" Jonathan asked.

I shrugged. "I think he wants to murder you either way."

He nodded. "Seems about right."

"He wanted me to give Walrum all the information he would need to convince you that he is regaining his memories. Then, as I assume he did today, he remembered bits and pieces that can help put him in jail. That way, at the trial, all the head admirals would be there. The backup was me confessing everything. Technically he didn't need me to do that, but Rolf here decided to push his buttons."

Rolf gave me a wink. "You said to use any means necessary."

"That I did. But still, I didn't think you would go that far. Anyway, so half the information Walrum has said was given to him by Sebastien and the other half me."

"So he doesn't actually have any of his memories."

I shook my head. "No. He doesn't. That person is no longer Walrum. I don't think his soul is in there any longer."

"And then what? Why does he want the trial to go forward?"

"There are a lot of people on his side—a lot who will profit from a war between nations. Their goal is to cause chaos here and move across the border to YamaXie and help them set up an army."

All of them stared at me like I was surprising them. None of this should have been that astonishing. Rolf was the first to speak. "So he is going to kill everyone there?"

I nodded. "Wants to, anyway."

"So we need to make that impossible." Jonathan rubbed the scruff on his face.

"But you don't know who is on his side. I don't even know. The only way to survive it is to make sure all head officials are wearing bulletproof vests and that no one who doesn't need to be there is gone." I shrugged. "I was going to do just that, but now I'm here so this is all up to you. What do you all want to do here?"

The three of them glanced at each other. Rolf bit his lip. "This isn't going to be an easy task. Anything we instigate will get back to those who are in charge."

"Although it is horrible, the best course of action would just make sure the admirals and any captains have vests on. We can assume most of them aren't behind it. Make sure they are armed and at the ready," I explained. "Anyone else will just get caught in the crossfire."

"That is one way of going about it. We will relay this information to Bardon. Meanwhile, if I see any inclination that you trying to let Sebastien know..." Rolf eyed me.

"Then you can go ahead and kill me." I smiled. "I don't ever want to actually be helping him ever again."

"What is the end goal here then?" Nik asked. "Will Sebastien be trying to escape?"

I nodded. "Yeah. And if he does and takes me with him, I can guarantee I'll finish him off myself."

Rolf checked his watch. "We need to get out of here. If anything comes up, we will get you what you need somehow. Meanwhile, just act your normal cocky self."

"I'll try." I turned to Nik. "Just promise me you'll watch your back, okay?"

He nodded. "I will." Nik leaned in and kissed me on the lips. His lips were soft against mine.

"And make sure Walrum, or whatever he is, doesn't get any information that isn't needed," I added. "He's as dangerous as he was when we found him."

With that, they left me in my cell. I collapsed back on my bed, careful to lay back exactly where I had been when I woke up. Hopefully a change would be seen as a glitch on the monitor when the camera turned back on.

CHAPTER THIRTY-TWO

Nik

The trial day was here. Jonathan, Bardon, Jørgensen, and I had worked hard at figuring out how we would go about making sure people were safe without causing a stir. Normally, with any other trial, there wasn't much worry that someone would attack since we were on a military base. But that all changed since it was Sebastien who was on trial.

We had on our vests under our military uniforms that we had to wear for this trial, and the four of us had guns at the ready. As for the admirals, they too were informed to wear their armor in case anything happened. There were fifteen admirals who were attending of the twenty-four. As long as half showed, the trial could be performed, and the admirals were the jury, in a sense. Being a military trial, it followed a few different rules than one a normal citizen would go through. Let's just say, it could be in some ways a lot less fair. But Sebastien didn't deserve fair. Not after everything he had done.

I sat next to Jonathan. We would have to go up and speak eventually if all this got that far. Neither of us were sure how long it would be before they would try to attack. There would be no point in getting that far—it would just be a waste of everyone's time. Once everyone was settled, I had a feeling that would be when the action started.

So good thing Jonathan and I replaced every guard's gun with blanks.

They were extra heavy blanks too, so they wouldn't feel the difference. There were still knives about, and the admirals had guns, and of course we did, but those were a lot easier to handle. We just prayed none of the other admirals were in on this.

The room got set up as people came in from all parts of the base. As the room was filling up, a few familiar faces stepped in.

"I didn't realize the crew we worked with was coming here for this."

Jonathan nodded. "Yup, they barely made it on time. Burt notified them, and they wanted to help Alexandra with her testimony."

"That could make this a bit more complicated."

"Yup, but I couldn't really tell them no without people being suspicious."

The room filled up, and Mary, Russ, and Samuel all went and sat with Burt and Alexandra. I would have to keep an eye on them. They were young and didn't deserve to be a part of this life.

Guards brought in Walrum and Rebecca. Rebecca was, of course, in cuffs, but Walrum was not, due to them thinking he was fine. I cursed under my breath.

"If he is as good of a fighter as Walrum once was, this is going to be one fun trial," Jonathan commented.

"Let's just pray it doesn't come down to having to take him out."

"I lost hope a while ago. Now I just plan out worst-case scenarios and go from there."

That was definitely fair after all this. The two of them, along with the mercenaries and doctors who had been brought in for questioning, were taken to another part of the room. The doors opened again, and the entire room went silent as Sebastien, dressed in his admiral uniform, grinned as he was ushered over to the lone table he would stand at.

That is, until he tried to murder us all.

"Can we just kill him now and be over with it?" I asked in a whisper.

Jonathan shook his head. "Unfortunately, we cannot. Otherwise, we will be on trial."

Rebecca was frowning as she glared at Sebastien. She hated him as much as the rest of us—if not more. I couldn't wait to see his plan fall apart because of what she confessed. Then he would see she was not just some tool for him to use.

Admiral Bardon stood up from his chair. "Admiral Sebastien Wilde. You are on trial for committing war crimes against humanity—for going against the T.O.W.E.R. How do you plead?"

Sebastien held up his cuffed hands. "Guilty."

The entire room flooded with noise. Sebastien began to laugh as suddenly the entire place began to shake and the section behind the admirals exploded.

Jonathan and I took cover as shards of the table and wall filled the area. I expected bullets to rain down upon us, but there was no noise. It was only aimed at the admirals.

I prayed that Bardon was all right. With the vests on, they should be, for the most part, all right. They were heavy duty—a lot more shielding than they had been in past wars. The explosion wasn't that large, and we had survived a lot worse.

I turned back to find a handful of the guards rushing in to guard Sebastien. Those were the ones who betrayed us. They unbound his wrists and handed him a gun. I prayed to *Gott* that was one of the ones that were filled with blanks.

Rebecca got herself released. I didn't know if one of the guards did it or she did it herself, as getting out of cuffs was her specialty. She grabbed a gun from one of the guards, along with a knife.

Well, at least I knew one of those would work to protect her.

Jonathan and I pulled out our own tranquilizer guns and aimed at the guards surrounding Sebastien. We didn't want them to die as we needed to find out how

Sebastien was controlling them. We took down two as Sebastien spun around and saw us. He grinned a little.

"Ah, my old captains. I see you were ready for something bad to happen. Well done."

"Hands where we can see them!" Jonathan ordered as he pulled out his pistol.

Sebastien nodded behind us. "Maybe you should make sure those crewmates of yours don't get killed when you aren't looking."

Both of us glanced behind ourselves to find Walrum heading toward where Alexandra and the others were. They tried to make a run for it, but Alexandra was too slow. Walrum grabbed her and stabbed his knife straight in her throat.

"No!" I screamed.

CHAPTER THIRTY-THREE

Rebecca

My attention had been on Sebastien, so I hadn't realized Walrum had made his way toward Alexandra. I watched as blood sprayed across the chairs. There was no way she was going to survive that. Jonathan and Nik ran to her but it was too late.

I stood there, stunned, as people screamed and panicked, trying to leave the trial. I couldn't believe my eyes. Even with warning, this was all going down shit creek.

And I was the one to blame.

I shook the thought off. No, this wasn't my fault. There was no reason that this should have gone the way it did. Sebastien had to have known I spilled information to the rest.

Turning my attention back to him, I aimed the gun and pulled the trigger.

The gun made a loud sound, but Sebastien didn't go down. He turned, hearing the noise, and grinned as he headed my way.

I shot again and again. It was full of blanks. Of course, that made sense. That was why there weren't bullets raining everywhere even though it was full of gunshot sounds. Bardon had made it so only they had the real guns. How could I be so stupid and so fucking screwed?

Pulling out my knife, I slashed at him as he made his way near me. He grabbed my wrist, ready for my attack, and grabbed my other arm.

"You, little *Zicke*, are coming with me." He struggled with my arms and forced me to drop the knife.

"No! You *Schwein*! Let me go!"

I tried to fight with him, but he was stronger than I was. I watched as Walrum grabbed Mary—the young mechanic from our earlier mission. Walrum held her in front of us as guards cleared a path for us. Mary was screaming and crying as Walrum held his knife in front of her throat.

"Sebastien! Stop now or we will shoot!" Jonathan warned as he stepped closer to us.

Sebastien turned and twisted me in front of him. "Go ahead, but you'll be sending her to hell with me."

"Do it!" I yelled. "Just kill me too!"

Jonathan and Nik hesitated long enough to where one of the guards smacked Jonathan in the back of the head. Nik turned around and shot him with his gun.

Sebastien took the opportunity to flee with me fighting him the entire way to the helicopter jet with Walrum right behind, dragging Mary along.

"Let her go. It's me who you want!" I yelled as he pulled us on board.

Sebastien slapped me, and I hit the floor of the helicopter jet. I tasted blood.

"I need her to make sure you follow instructions, now don't I?"

Walrum and Mary got on, and the vehicle flew up in the air. I dragged myself over to Mary, whose eyes were red with tears.

"It will be okay," I whispered to her. "It will be okay."

CHAPTER THIRTY-FOUR

Nik

It took twenty minutes to finally subdue all the guards who helped Sebastien escape. I had no idea why they would serve someone who would just abandon them like he did, but I supposed we would find that out after we questioned them all.

Besides a giant lump on his head, Jonathan ended up all right. Of all the admirals, only a couple were critically injured and were sent to the hospital. The armor that everyone was asked to wear came in handy, as the armor was made for blasts as well. The only problem was that they were knocked out for a bit and couldn't use their guns, which made everything a lot harder.

Sebastien's goal was to take out as many admirals as he could before fleeing with that bomb, but it had failed. He was able to take Rebecca with him, and the face she made as she was dragged out of there made my heart darken. Sebastien had managed to get away with her and Mary, and we were trying to track how he was getting to YamaXie. Burt and Russ were with Jonathan and me, going through visual logs and databases, trying to find anything that they could.

Bardon stepped in the room, the cuts on his face now bandaged. Behind him was Jørgensen, who had a gash across his nose and a black eye.

Bardon began, "We tried everything we could, but Alexandra is gone. There was too much blood lost by the time medics reached her. She was already dead."

I shook my head. None of this was fair. Sebastien was going to pay, if it was the last thing I did.

Thank You For Reading!

Thank you so much for reading! Readers like you make it possible for authors like me to write stories! If you could spare a moment and leave a review on Amazon, Goodreads, BookBub, and wherever you like to buy books, that would mean the world to me! It really helps authors like me to succeed in the publishing world.

Book 3 is coming Winter 2021!

<u>Acknowledgements</u>

I want to thank everyone who helped me with this novel! This series all started at ASU's Your Novel Year Program back in 2015. I want to say thank you to my mentors Mike, Joe, Chantelle, Kevin, and Paul who helped me with all my writing questions and taught me how to write. Thank you to everyone in the program who gave me feed back (dad, Cassie, Gil, Gina, Jeff, Laura, Marcel, Stacy, Deborah, Paul, Jasmine, and Tom), and to my writing group who also helped with this project (Traci, Rebecca, Bernie, and Christi). Thank you to my editor Anne Victory and cover artist Biserka Designs who made this book possible. Thank you to Kaleb who answered all my random questions. I swear it was for a book! Another thank you to my friends Earlene, Shayne, Faye, Veronica, Tom, Carl, Ruben, Justin, and all the others who have helped with this book over the years. Lastly, thank you to my parents who have always supported me, and to my husband who gets the privilege of reading all my books :).

About the Author

Lyra Thorsson is the sci-fi pen name for Dani Hoots. She is a science fiction, fantasy, romance, and young adult author who loves anything with a story. She has a B.S. in Anthropology, a Masters of Urban and Environmental Planning, a Certificate in Novel Writing from Arizona State University, and a BS in Herbal Science from Bastyr University.

Her hobbies include reading, watching anime, cooking, studying different languages, wire walking, hula hoop, and working with plants. She is also an herbalist and sells her concoctions on FoxCraft Apothecary. She lives in Phoenix with her husband and visits Seattle often.

Feel free to email her with any questions you might have!
danihootsauthor@gmail.com